ALWAYS THADDEUS

Marcee Corn

ARCHWAY
PUBLISHING

This is a work of fiction. All of the characters, names, incidents, organizations, and dialogue in this novel are either the products of the author's imagination or are used fictitiously.

Archway Publishing books may be ordered through booksellers or by contacting:

Archway Publishing
1663 Liberty Drive
Bloomington, IN 47403
www.archwaypublishing.com
1 (888) 242-5904

ISBN: 978-1-4808-4825-2 (sc)
ISBN: 978-1-4808-4930-3 (hc)
ISBN: 978-1-4808-4824-5 (e)

Library of Congress Control Number: 2017909069

Print information available on the last page.

Archway Publishing rev. date: 6/28/2017

For Rob

Without your continued patience, support, suggestions, edits and love,
I could not have written this novel. Thank you. I love you.

ACKNOWLEDGMENTS

First and foremost, I want to thank my wonderful husband, Rob. His overwhelming support and encouragement of my crazy idea of writing a mystery novel is astounding. During all the hours I spent in front of the computer, he didn't complain; in fact, he encouraged. His ideas, editing skills, the words for the poem titled *The Accounting,* and the dialogue suggestions helped me complete *Always Thaddeus.* Most importantly, I thank you, Rob, for sharing your life with me. I love you.

Secondly, I want to thank my amazing and creative children. Bailey, Spencer, and Peter. Your continued support, words of encouragement, and advice on the storyline kept me moving forward with this endeavor. I pray you will always follow your passions and dreams. I am blessed to call you my children. I love you.

I would like to thank my amazing friend, Jeff Freels. I can still see the four of us - you, Amy, Rob and me – sitting around the fire on that snowy evening as I shared my story of *Thaddeus* with you. You were amazing as you got up and started pacing around the room getting increasingly excited about the plot and pitching your imaginative ideas, especially for the ending. Your creative genius helped to make *Always Thaddeus* the story that it is.

My special thanks goes to Jill C. Corley, my amazing editor. She is a most talented wordsmith and has an eagle eye for mistakes, punctuation, and word choice. Oh, and pronouns, I won't forget all the work you did with the pronouns! Ha! Thank you, my friend, for your expertise.

So many thanks to the talented UK artist, James Mackenzie, for collaborating with me on this project. Your vibrant artwork, *Sea Storm at Sunset,* is an amazing cover for *Always Thaddeus.* The black and white sketches you created for the inside of the book are perfect especially since you have never been to Maine. Thank you, my friend, for sharing your talent with my readers.

Lastly, my sincere thanks go to a group of seven special women - The Mag 8 - Sheri, Sue, Jill, Tink, Joy, Annelisa and Theresa. You were my support group, and more importantly, my very creative band of authors, editors, and brilliant friends that encouraged and advised me during the writing and promotion of *Always Thaddeus*. Thank you, my beautiful friends.

CONTENTS

PART ONE

PART TWO

SNEAK PREVIEW - ALWAYS THADDEUS BOOK TWO

PART ONE

PROLOGUE

Beth Morgan sits alone on the porch of the funeral home. She slowly rocks herself back and forth and back again, searching for comfort.

The sound of the old rocking chair does not provide it.
Her husband attempts to bring it, though he is not able.
And the hordes of people around her, are just that...a horde.

Alone in her misery, Beth sits and rocks herself back and forth and back again.

Questions whirl around in her head as if in a cesspool of hopelessness.

They say on the day that Thad died, he went to heaven.
Did he?
They say it was a peaceful death.
Was it?
They say he was in no pain.
How do *they* know?
They say I could hold my boy just one more time, before he goes to heaven.
So I did.
I held him for a long time.

Then...
They took him away... away from my arms.
Away from me, his mother.
They say I will heal in time.
But I won't.

They say that I can have more children after his death.
But I can't.
They say all these things and more to me.
But I stop listening.

I am tired of listening to what *they* say.
I am tired of them.

They are noise. Like cymbals crashing, they distract me from my search for comfort, and more importantly, peace.
They don't understand.
And worse, Andrew doesn't understand.

Beth searches the scrapbook of her mind for every image of Thad she can hold on to, begging for peace. She becomes fully aware that she will no longer be able to hold her son. No longer will she hear his sweet voice. And no longer will he need her. She won't be able to push him on a swing or play ball with him or watch him grow up. He will be out of reach and that is not acceptable to her or her sanity.

Like a drowning victim at sea, Beth is desperate. Floundering in deep waves of sadness, she attempts to reach out for a lifesaver. But where is it? She retreats further into her mind to fervently dig into the abyss for something she can hold on to. She leaves reason behind, and crawls into a cave of denial and into the depths of her soul. There her thoughts become her only comfort, and the voice in her mind, her only friend. The preserver of her sanity must reside in a new reality.

On that day, the day of Thad's death, Beth stops listening to what *they* say…she stops believing in what *they* believe. She listens to only one voice now. That one voice is the voice that takes up residency in her mind. It is the voice of counterfeit comfort and peace. It is the voice of artificial safety. It's a very special voice that is born on the day Thad dies.

This secret inner voice tells her that those things that "*they*" told her are not true. The voice tells her that Thaddeus is out there. He is not gone. All she has to do is search hard enough for him. The voice tells her that she will be able to be with her son again. And he will call her Mommy. This is her reality.

On the day of Thaddeus' death, Beth allows the calming voice to take over. The secret voice that whispers its message to her over and over as it penetrates her being, becoming the motivation that she needs to survive.

Two days later, Beth greets the mourners on the steps of the large Methodist Church begrudgingly wearing the appropriate black hat and somber dress. Contrary to her attire, she also wears a simple smile on her face and slight glint in her eyes. The hordes can't know it, her husband doesn't know it, but hope has found her. Though there is a tombstone with her son's name on it, Beth believes with all her heart that Thaddeus is still alive. All she must do now… is find him.

Setting out on her mission she travels to a neighboring town; Beth has some important business to tend to.

She enters the shop with a mission and a certainty. She quietly lays back in the reclining chair to let the professional do his job. The dark haired beauty closes her eyes and dreams of Thaddeus.

She wakes to an unfamiliar voice in her ear saying,

"I am finished."

Opening her eyes she feels pain. But this pain is not the sorrowful one found in her broken heart, it is a good pain. It has purpose.

Looking to her left arm, the blood is puddled up between and around the words etched there. These are words that she would live by. These are the words from her mind that had quietly taken up residency in her heart. And now too, were in permanent black ink on her forearm.

Beth's broken heart skips a beat as she mouths the words there, *Always Thaddeus*. For the first time in several days, she smiles. Pulling her sleeve down she sets off on her search. This mission will consume Beth for the rest of her life.

CHAPTER I

The Island

As the late summer sun falls lower in the afternoon sky, the hour approaches for her arrival. Eager anticipation fills Andrew as if he were back in sixth grade and going on his first date.

"She's coming today!" he says aloud to Toby, his oversized "shotgun riding" mutt. Surprised by the volume of his own voice echoing in the cab of his truck, he looks to his best friend for reassurance. "How do I look, ole fella?"

Toby tilts his head in Andrew's direction and shows his teeth.

"Thanks bud! I'll take that as, 'You look quite debonair, sexy, and most handsome, my man.'" He laughs and rubs Toby roughly under his chin.

Andrew continues, "Her ride from the mainland ought to be a smooth one. The weather couldn't be better with blue skies and a slight north wind. The water is glass today. The oversized ferry hull will slide right through it with ease."

Wondering why he sounds exactly like Ray, the local weatherman, rattling off the water conditions on the early morning news channel, he is interrupted for a brief moment by Sandy's smiling face. Realizing that his mind-portrait paints a much younger face than he will see today, he returns to his more immediate concerns - the nagging questions that are accompanied by unknown answers.

Will I be able to draw on those feelings of the past? Or will we be strangers who once knew each other?

Do I really know how I feel?
No, not really.

Do we really know each other?
No, not really.

Was it foolish for me to ask her here?
No, not really.

Like Toby, Andrew stares out the front window, not knowing the answers.

The drive over to the ferry mooring is a short one. And for that he is glad. He is more nervous than he ever thought he would be meeting Sandy after all these years. Andrew passes Joe's Crab and Lobster Shack with the attached bait shop on his way.

He looks over to see the usual crowd of locals sitting in their customary spots, along with a couple of tourists who have joined them outside on the picnic benches. Andrew is sure they are discussing the terrible shape the world is in or how good or bad the crabbin' or fishin' had been that day. It was always the same conversations with the same guys sharing the same opinions.

It's a "fishermen-only" kind of imaginary club where the rules are etched in their brains, just as they were with their fathers before them. Always the same, and 'sameness' is what Andrew likes. As expected, they wave or nod as his truck rattles along the dirt road beside them. And just as typically, he nods back.

Andrew feels the chill in the air teasing of the approaching winter. Soon it will be time to batten down the cottage and head south. He notes the coolness but does not want to acknowledge that his days on the island are numbered. He loves this place along with the Mainers who make their homes here.

Not surprisingly, two of those people, Sue and Samuel are out in their small garden in front of their wind-blown shingled cottage digging in the beds with their usual attention to detail. Their flowers are the prettiest on the island and they know it. Andrew stops the truck as he typically does. The pair cease their digging and look in his direction.

"What's happening, Sam and Sue?" Andrew yells, as they both are hard of hearing.

"Oh, not much" Samuel yells back. "Just out here diggin' and piddlin' with my beautiful bride!" He always calls Sue his beautiful bride. And his answer is always the same, "Just out here diggin' and piddlin' with my beautiful bride!"

"Aren't you a sight for sore eyes Andrew Morgan?" Sue beams.

Smiling, he thinks for a second about asking them for one of their pink roses to give to Sandy when she arrives, but then decides better of it and says, "Your roses are as beautiful and as fragrant as ever. I always enjoy their scent as I ride by."

"Where are you going so late in the afternoon?" Samuel asks.

"Oh, I am going to the ferry to pick up a friend who will be visiting for a few days," Andrew sheepishly answers back.

With that, Sue looks out from under her wide-brimmed hat, getting totally engaged in the conversation. She smiles in a devilish way. "You have a gooooood visit with her now, ya hear, Andrew?" mocking his Tennessee accent as she talks. "Make every moment count, dear," she adds.

He nods his head as he stores away her wise words somewhere in his brain. Smiling, he knows why he loves that old gal. She knows him better than anyone else around here and even better than his own mother. It seems he never has to say much and she knows just what is going on in his head.

"I got to be on my way now! I don't wanna be late! I will bring her round to see you in the next few days." Andrew shouts as he starts up his old truck again.

"Okay now," they both say in unison, turning to get back to their gardening.

Waving, he heads on down the road, leaving behind the hunched-over pair in his rearview mirror.

As Andrew drives away, he realizes once again how much he adores this island and the people here. It is his home now, his forever home, and he couldn't be happier that he found this special place. It had been a long time coming. If the winters didn't force him to go, he would never leave this quiet, simple place.

The winters on Owl's Nest are fierce. No, "fierce" does not describe them, he decides. It is the possibility of death. The nor'easters blow with a vengeance in the winter forcing the few remaining islanders to hunker down in their homes with no relief from the cold, howling winds, snow, and ice.

Andrew had spent part of his first winter on Owl's Nest, living the solitary life of a hermit, which he is certain he will never do again. If he could have vacated, he would have. But because he was not a Mainer, the ferry was his only way off the island, and as he found out the hard way, it doesn't run in the winter. If he had known the mailman he could have caught a ride with him on the mail boat, which ran three days a week, but Andrew didn't know him back then. So, without a sturdy boat or knowledge of the mailman, he was stuck. But most folks knew this and evacuated the small island in the fall.

That first winter, Andrew was stuck. He was left behind with his dog, a pile of firewood and a pantry full of canned food. He still remembers how miserable he was. The cold wind ripped through his cottage finding every crack and crevice it could squeeze through, never letting up. The sound of it was utterly frightening and the cold of it was downright paralyzing. He had never been as damp, cold, and lonely as he was that winter.

Because of that first horrible winter, he usually plans to leave early in November, catching a ride with a local fisherman or friend to the mainland. The ferry quits running in October. Most of the tourists and summer folks have gone by then and the permanent islanders are left. They are a small band of folks, a tough, hardy group, but his favorite kind of folks. Sue and Samuel are two of those people.

As Andrew rounds the bend in the road and comes off the rise, he can see the ferry pulling into the harbor below him. It is loaded down with SUVs carrying kayaks, bicycles, children, adults and their pets. It is late August and families still have the last remnants of vacation time left. He is glad that Sandy is on that ferry, enjoying the first sites of his beloved island.

From the boat, the island looks extremely small. But that is an illusion; and the truth is only made visible by time and exploration. The harbor is small and most of the boats are anchored out in the bay. The tide recedes too far to allow boats to remain at the dock. The ferry only arrives at high tide, and its mooring is dredged out every year.

There is a quaint old building painted bright red sitting near the dock. This tired- looking structure greets all the visitors from the mainland, and bids them a hearty welcome to Maine. Hanging all over the four sides of the building are hundreds of aged buoys draped with fishing nets reminding visitors of the island's rich history. It is very charming. On any given day when the sun is out, tourists can see an artist or two set up with his easel on the hill, painting that old building that sits beside the sea with the beaten rocky coast below. There are probably hundreds of paintings of that old ziggurat out there somewhere; reminders of what Maine is supposed to be: harbors, lobster boats, ferries, rugged ocean and rocks. Sandy will love it, Andrew is sure.

CHAPTER 2

Ferry Ride

As the old ferryboat shutters to a stop, adults aboard excitedly gather their children and pets and pile back into their vehicles to disembark. Sandy too, waits in her car, hands on the steering wheel, anticipating her turn to leave the ferry. Her heart skips a beat as she releases her brake. She inches her car forward as she scans along the bank for some sign that Andrew is there.

The other cars, trucks, bicycles, and walkers parade off the boat. She follows, clanking down the metal ramp and then slowly moving onto the shore. It is an unpleasant sound with all the banging, rattling and scraping, but it only lasts a few moments and then it is over. Sandy is relieved that she is finally on her way up the ramp leaving that awful sound as well as her stale life behind. She is ready for a new adventure and Andrew could be just the man to share it with.

Making her way along the gravel incline to the main road, she continues looking for him. The massive red barn-like building to her right momentarily distracts her. Being a sucker for nautical and old things she slows her car to have a better look. It has been a long time since she has been to New England. This island is exactly what she remembered of the area and had pictured in her mind.

As she takes in the scene along with a deep and much needed breath, she also admires the shingled old houses sitting proudly along the shore enduring the test of countless seasons. She is glad she came.

The sky is sapphire and the ocean a calm, deeper gray; colors that only the seashore can bring. Small boats bobbing up and down in the slight waves grab her attention as she watches them nod in her direction. It is as if they are saying, "Welcome to Owl's Nest, Sandy." She accepts their greeting and slowly nods back keeping tempo with the rhythm of the sea. Life just seems to take a step back in time here, she thinks, and perhaps that is the reason Andrew wanted her to come.

Sandy continues to look around her, still noticing the simplicity of her surroundings. She spots Andrew sitting on a knoll. He sits amongst the tall grass watching and waiting for her. He is leaning against a roached out old pickup truck with his knees up and his tanned arms resting comfortably across them. Pulled down to his eyebrows and covering most of his hair, sits a New York Yankees baseball cap. His sunglasses hang on its brim. He wears an old pair of khakis and a faded Emerson, Lake and Palmer t-shirt that looks to be his favorite. He doesn't see her yet, so she pulls her car over into the tall grass quite a ways from where he sits. She allows herself another minute of time to gather herself and calm her pounding heart before approaching him.

Andrew remains a handsome man, older of course, and kind of weathered-looking...but handsome nonetheless. Her heart flutters within the hammering as she keeps watching him. He has wrinkles around his sea blue eyes which gaze into the distance towards the ramp, searching. His beard is kept and growing white in some places, and his forearms are tanned and muscular. He seems to add near perfect life to a perfect landscape.

CHAPTER 3

Reunited

Surprised, Andrew notices Sandy sitting in her car not ten feet in front of him. Just as his eyes meet hers, he cannot control the wide smile that rips across his face. He hops up from where he is resting and quickly walks towards her. She climbs out of her car and meets him at her car door just as she is closing it.

They cautiously embrace as he speaks to her in his slow and familiar southern drawl, "Hey Sandy Smithson. Did 'ya have a good trip?"

"It was wonderful, she beamed. "It's just so beautiful here, Andrew, I can see why you love it so."

He looks out into the harbor and shakes his head agreeing with her, as his arms squeeze her thin frame tightly. The hug he gives her is a little rougher than he intends, and he begins to feel uncomfortable as he hopes he hadn't squeezed her too intensely. He notices that she seems to have lost her breath for a minute. Realizing that it has been way too long since he has hugged a woman and feeling uneasy about it, Andrew lets loose of her quickly as she takes a much-needed breath.

Self-conscious, he promptly turns away from her and heads towards his truck motioning her to follow him. Left with a wildly beating heart, Sandy turns and hops back into her waiting car as to not be left behind.

Andrew shakes his head as he jumps into his truck realizing that he just made a fool of himself with Sandy. "Calm down, you old fool." He tells himself and Toby. "She is just an old friend...a beautiful old friend."

Sandy can't keep the smile off of her face as she bounces along the road behind his truck. Her heart remembers the feeling from all those years ago…a feeling she hadn't felt in a very long time.

As the two slowly drive down the somewhat pitted gravel road, the sun continues to melt into the sea. It is a beautiful sight and Sandy can hardly keep her eyes on the road, wanting to gaze out towards the ocean to see the setting sun. The pinks and oranges in the sky are so vivid that everything around her picks up the hue. As the road winds its way along the water, little cottages with glorious flowerbeds line the street on either side.

Within a matter of minutes, the sun completely submerges into the water, leaving the ocean a darker purplish gray as the bright colors of the day quickly fade. With the water suddenly becoming cold and foreboding to her, Sandy shivers just as a gust of air blows a cooler breeze into her car window. She pulls her sweater around her, not wanting to roll up the window.

The road makes its way along the shore for a good piece, and then turns sharply off the water's edge up a winding road into a dark, wooded place. Tall pine trees hang over the road and Sandy feels the need to turn on her headlights to see. The lane becomes less traveled and more pitted as they make their way leaving the town and cottages behind them. Her car bumps along the deserted and desolate road traveling uphill until they pull into a clearing. Quite without warning, the road suddenly ends as a simple, weathered cottage blocks the way. Sandy pulls up beside Andrew's truck in front of the cottage and turns off her car.

With the darkness of the forest behind her, her eyes and ears can now feast on the site of the sky, and the vast open ocean before her. Andrew's cottage is perched on a bluff surrounded on three sides by the massive, almost violent sea. The sound of the rushing sea crashing on the rocks below is overwhelming.

The sun is no more, but its dim yellows and glimmers of orange light remain in the western sky, reflecting into the dark water below. The sound of the breaking ocean waves and the sight of the tangerine sky leave her completely speechless. With Sandy's eyes trained on the beautiful and mesmerizing view, she can only sit.

Andrew brings her mind back to reality as he asks for her keys to get her suitcase out of the trunk. She hands them to him through her open window, still in a daze. Giant dog paws shake the car and Sandy from her present state, as the goofy head attached to those paws fills her car window.

"Well, hello there big guy." Sandy says to Toby.

She reaches out to pat the top of his head not quite sure if he will allow her or not.

About that time, Andrew comes from around the back of the car with her suitcase, yelling at the dog to get down.

"Well, are you going to sit there all night?" Andrew says with a smile as Toby runs ahead of him to the front door.

"Oh, no, of course not." Sandy blushes at him as she opens her car door.

"...And who is this?" she asks pointing to Toby.

"That big mutt is Toby, my best friend in all the world. Toby, meet Sandy, one of my oldest and dearest friends."

As if on cue, Toby does as Andrew suggests and walks over to meet Sandy. He smells the hem of her skirt then circles around her sniffing loudly as he goes. After a long moment, seemingly satisfied, he licks her bare leg, and lets her pass.

Sandy learns later that Andrew and Toby are quite the duo. Toby was a mutt of sorts-large and clumsy, and nothing but skin and bones when he found him. Andrew had been exploring around his property when he first moved in and was checking out the big barn up in the meadow when he heard a sad, whimpering noise coming from inside. Toby was huddled back in the corner, sick, scared and starving. Andrew rescued him from certain doom that day by nursing him back to health. Toby has never forgotten it and neither has Andrew, because that was the day both of their hearts started to love again.

Opening the door of his cottage Andrew steps back to let Sandy enter first, telling Toby to sit and wait. She goes into the warm room. The front door of the cottage opens into a large open space. A small kitchen is on one wall of the room near the front door, and a long antique harvest table and eight chairs on the other. Beyond the open space, she can see a sitting area with a large floor to ceiling fireplace on one entire wall surrounded by lovely walnut bookcases filled with hundred of books. The sky and ocean view lay beyond the row of windows along the back of the room.

A door to a porch separating the windows on either side is open allowing the cool ocean breezes to enter the screen door. The entire room is wood...from the floor to the ceiling and in between bathing the cottage in warmth and creating an inviting atmosphere. Over-stuffed furniture wrapped in worn leather decorates the room. A large oval braided rug fills the floor. Off to the right side of the dining area is a long hallway, which Andrew proceeds down with her suitcase in hand. He turns into a room on the left. Sandy follows.

Once again, as she enters the small room, Sandy is struck by the view of the sea from the windows. The bedroom is on the back of the cottage facing the sea. It is cozy with a big brass bed taking up most of the space, and an antique dresser and mirror filling the rest of it. Andrew switches on the lamp on the dresser, and puts her suitcase on the cushioned window seat. The floor is polished to a shine and the bed looks to be soft and comfortable with its layered blankets, more pillows than a single person needs, and a faded hand stitched quilt. A small fireplace sits on the closest wall to the door. A fire has been laid and he takes a long match out of a box on the mantle and lights the paper. The dry wood begins to crackle and burn almost instantly. A warm glow fills the space.

Andrew turns to leave her room, and smiles as he tells her, "I hope you will be comfortable here. If there is anything you need, just let me know. I am so glad you came, Sandy."

Smiling warmly, she responds with a sigh, "Yeah, me too."

Sandy walks over to the window seat, opens her suitcase and grabs a bottle of wine that she brought to thank him for his hospitality. She set it on the dresser so that she doesn't forget to give it to him when she goes back into the kitchen. Looking out towards the ocean she sees that the view is almost absent from her now except for the deep purple sky hovering over the black surface of the water. She remembers seeing that exact same purple sky one dreary winter day in Nashville many years before. Suddenly, she becomes a prisoner in her own mind as she pauses to remember the last time she saw Andrew. It had to have been nearly ten years ago.

On that day, Sandy met Andrew on the stone steps of the First United Methodist Church in downtown Nashville on a cold and bleak winter day as she was attempting to slip inside unnoticed. The two only spoke for a moment, greeting each other with a hug. Sandy's heart sank as she could see and feel the absolute sadness etched on Andrew's face. His young son, Thad, had died quite suddenly from an unexpected illness. Somehow, Andrew found Sandy living in McMinnville and called to let her know. Two days later, she jumped in her car and bolted to Nashville during a terrible storm to attend the boy's funeral.

A lovely, tall, dark-haired woman was at Andrew's side on the church steps, holding and tending to a baby wrapped tightly in pink blankets. Andrew introduced Beth as his wife, and thanked Sandy for coming. With that introduction Beth smiled at her, turned, and walked off to greet other mourners already inside the church. Sandy remembered telling Andrew how very sorry she was and that he had a beautiful daughter.

His only comment that day to her was, "Thank you so much for coming. I will miss my son, Thad, and that is not my daughter."

Sandy left the church, after the funeral that day unable to speak to Andrew again as his wife, the dark-haired beauty, never left his side.

Sandy didn't hear from Andrew again until his unexpected call that came a week ago when he invited her to Owl's Nest...his retreat in Maine. She had been surprised that he did, but even more surprised when she heard herself answer, "Sure, I would love to, Andrew."

CHAPTER 4

Train Ride

As the train engine pulls away from the station, Beth is glad to finally be sitting. She is tired. She looks down at her hands as they tightly grasp her overstuffed bag that sits across her lap. Her white-knuckled hands clutch her only belongings in this world with a vice-like grip...a relic of an old habit that somehow she can't escape.

Still looking at her hands, she admires the only valuable possession she has, her mother's ring. She had learned from the nuns at the orphanage that her mother, Jackie, had tied it into a tiny bundle of fabric and had stuffed it into her pocket on the day she left her. Beth guarded that ring with her life because it was from her mother, a woman she had no memory of.

Desperately trying to change her life for the better, Beth had boarded this particular train spending a good portion of the little bit of money she had left. She planned to travel to Nashville, Tennessee in hopes of making a positive change to her path and eventually to her life. Not long ago, she found out that Andrew Morgan was living and working there. Unbeknownst to him, she had fallen in love with him many years before. He still held a piece of her heart.

Peering through the grimy window Beth is fully aware that the filth there reflects her own life to this point. Rarely were there times in her twenty-three years where she could clearly see the path she should take...or even the fact that she had a choice in her path. She never looked forward to new situations mostly because the past proved them to be without hope and happiness. But it seems new situations always found her.

Riding on this train, she knows she is starting over once again. But this time the path she is on is one of her own choosing.

CHAPTER 5

Love in a Coal Town

Was Jackie a bad judge of character or was it that she desperately needed to find love and a better life? Whatever the answer, she fell deeply in love with Jordan Smithy, a selfish older man that saw her as an object that belonged to him.

Jordan traveled during the week selling coal for the Turner Brothers Coal Mine. Everyone in the small town where they lived worked for the Turners. Secretly, Jackie was glad when her husband was out of town. She could go to work at 'The Corner Diner', come home in the evening, worn out and tired, and enjoy some peace watching the TV programs she liked. When Jordan was home, her existence was nonexistence.

Her husband was a man of habit. He expected dinner to be ready at six o'clock on the dot. He only ate meat and potatoes and drank cheap beer. She had to have a homemade dessert ready on Fridays when he returned home at the end of the week. The house had to be clean and orderly, and most importantly, Jackie, was expected to look beautiful for him.

Jordan came in the front door at precisely five o'clock on Friday nights, pecked her on the cheek, and said to her, as if a broken record, "You look good enough to eat, doll." She always braced herself afterwards for the stinging slap he would plant on her bottom. He never asked her how her week had been or what she had done. He didn't really seem to care.

As if in a wretched movie that played over every Friday night, Jordan would throw down his bag at the door, sit in his chair and drink his cheap beer as he watched TV. Jackie would bring him his dinner at precisely six o'clock and place it on the TV tray that he pulled up beside his Lazy Boy. He watched his programs while eating his dinner, never noticing if she ate at all. And worst of all, he expected her to be happy, beautiful and eager for him that evening.

Their small house belonged to the Turners. They paid little rent since Jordan was one of their employees. This was appealing to him, as he was always obsessively saving money. So Jackie never felt like the house or anything in it was hers. Even her clothes were presents from Jordan so "his baby" could be dressed to perfection. He made sure she had the best clothes, finest jewelry, and anything else that made her appealing to him. Besides those things, everything else in the house was cheap and worn out.

All of Jordan's large family lived and worked in the sooty little town where the mine was located. The Smithy brothers all married local girls that they had known for their entire lives, all of them except Jordan. He was different. He was better. And the rest of the family thought so too.

When Jordan was eighteen years old, he started working on a business degree at the neighboring town's community college and finished night school in four years. He was the first one to get a degree in the Smithy family. During the day he was a coal miner alongside his daddy and brothers, but at night, he was a college student; something he was very proud of. His diploma from Strickland Community College still hangs in his parents' living room above their television, so the family can continue being proud.

Jackie had met Jordan Smithy in Providence, when he was on a business trip, two years before. He came into Stanley's Bar and Grill dressed sharply in a nice suit and tie and sat at the bar. She noticed him immediately and was attracted to the elegant looking older man sitting alone concentrating on his beer and the newspaper. She was there with friends enjoying a rare night out.

He had immediately noticed her beauty upon entering the bar and decided he had to have her. He bought her a drink and had it sent over to her table. Feeling like she was a heroine out of a novel, she stepped out of her comfort zone, realizing that perhaps he was her ticket out, and accepted the drink. When she had finished her martini, she walked over to his bar stool and quietly thanked him. He turned to her and invited her to sit with him at the bar. He was charming and witty.

"Please tell me your name." Jordan politely asked.

"My name is Jackie. What is yours?"

"I am Jordan Smithy. Nice to meet you, Jackie." With that greeting he shook her hand and smiled.

For the next thirty minutes, he asked all about her, focusing intently on all her answers. He bought her a second martini. When she asked about him, she found out that he had a college degree and a good job selling coal. He was a polished, older man and more confident than any man she had ever dated. These facts were very appealing to Jackie.

The two spent most of that first evening talking and drinking, and she quickly fell in love with him, his degree, and the possibilities of what could lie ahead for her if she was with him.

From their first meeting, Jordan was obsessed with her too. He didn't care that she was a waitress at a restaurant across town. He didn't care that she was only eighteen years old. He had already made up his mind that she would be his. Her long dark hair, smooth pale skin, red lips, big brown eyes and small curvy body were everything he had ever desired.

He came back into town and saw her often and they quickly became a couple. Jordan was not interested in dating Jackie; he wanted her for his own. So it wasn't long before they married.

Jackie was a runaway teen and had lived on her own since she was fifteen moving from place to place as she found work. So he was happy to fund the wedding and glad she didn't have a family to intervene.

Their wedding was a typical small town affair at his hometown church. Jordan picked out Jackie's wedding dress, the flowers, and the cake. The proud groom thought that Jackie was the most beautiful bride he had ever seen in the extremely low cut white silk gown that accentuated her tiny waist, large breasts, and rounded hips.

The reception was in the church basement Meeting Hall after the ceremony. All the locals came and ate cake, along with small mints and mixed nuts served on glass plates. The ginger ale punch complete with lime sherbet floating on the top was served in delicate teacups. The happy couple left soon after the reception, driving the short distance to the Holiday Inn on the coast for a two-day honeymoon.

She was happy then…mistaking Jordan's obsession for love.

His selfishness and tyranny strangled their marriage after the first month. For two long years, she succumbed to his every wish, day in and day out, hoping to keep him happy and pleased with her. She remained beautiful and desirable to him for those years, hoping he would change. He did not. Life for Jackie was quickly turning into misery.

Almost from the beginning of their marriage, she was a captive in her own home. Jordan only allowed her to go to work and back home again, riding the bus that picked her up in front of their house. She didn't have friends, as he wouldn't allow it. He was so afraid that he might lose his wife, his most prized possession that he built a tall fence around the backyard only allowing her to go out there during the day to tend to her beloved flower garden. She had to order the groceries by phone, and they could only be delivered when he was home. Jordan couldn't have been happier with his wife and life. He didn't need friends. He had Jackie.

She felt more and more trapped as her days passed and soon became desperate for a change. One day, she made a life altering decision. She would get pregnant. A child would surely bring about change to the monotonous life she lived with this man that she was beginning to detest.

She stopped taking her birth control pills without telling him. She knew that Jordan had planned for them to be married for five years before they would have their first child…and he had already decided that it would be a boy.

Six months after she quit taking the pill, Jackie became pregnant. She told Jordan the good news one cold Friday night as they were sipping wine and eating at the dining table, a rare treat.

"Jordan, honey, I have some good news for you." He looked up from his plate of food to listen to what his wife had to say. "We are pregnant! Isn't that exciting news?"

Upon hearing her tell him she was pregnant, Jordan immediately threw down his fork. It banged loudly on his almost empty china plate and bounced to the floor. He sat very still for what seemed like an eternity to Jackie staring into his wine glass. She began to get uneasy and didn't dare speak because she knew his anger was building.

His face grew redder as each minute ticked past. The silence unnerved her. His reaction to the news was not at all what she expected. Like a violent volcano suddenly awake, he began to spew words of hatred across the table at her, saying that she had no right to make such a decision without him and that she would pay dearly for her mistake.

To make his point even more dramatic, he threw the entire pot of stew that was sitting next to him across the dining room, almost hitting her in the face. Like his words, the stew spewed all over the wall and Jackie began to cry.

As Jordan was grabbing his coat and heading out the door, he screamed at his now-sobbing wife, "I will detest you for being fat. You better not be a lazy and a sick pregnant woman. I still expect the house to be perfect, my dinner to be ready at six every single night and of course, you will continue to work at the diner until that child is born!"

As if an after-thought, Jordan turned from the front door, stumbled back over to her chair where she was still sitting, pushed one of the other chairs out of his way and slammed it against the wall. Although Jordan had never hit her before, Jackie ducked her head to the table, expecting a blow. Instead, he pointed with his index finger at her stomach and jabbed his shaking finger into her abdomen.

Making a horribly distorted face, he screamed in her ear, "And most importantly, I don't want *that* baby, nor will I ever! This pregnancy *does not* fit into my plan! I hope *you* are happy, Jackie, 'cause *I am not*!" He turned from her and left the house. He didn't return for three weeks.

When Jordan finally returned home Jackie's life became even more unbearable. He stopped speaking to her, and he was much more demanding with what he wanted. Sometimes he wouldn't even come home on the weekends. She had no idea where he went or with whom.

As Jackie's belly grew with the child, his lack of desire for her did too. He didn't hold back the words of loathing he had for her growing girth calling it "ugly" and "gross". He stopped giving her nice clothes and jewelry; telling her that she had to make due with what she had. Jackie was miserable for the entire pregnancy. She realized then that this child growing in her belly was a mistake, a big mistake and she certainly *was* paying for it.

Finally the month came when the child was to be born. There was no baby bed, diapers, clothes or toys. Jackie had begged Jordan for those things and he had refused, saying, "You made the mistake, now live with it."

Their baby girl was born on a cold February morning in the Turner house in the bed where they slept. Jordan was out of town. Jackie was alone and desperate so she called her sister-in-law for help. The rest of the family knew how Jordan felt about the baby and had avoided him and Jackie like the plague for fear of his anger and most importantly his disappointment in them. But since he was out of town, the woman came with baby clothes, diapers, and clean blankets for the baby.

Jackie gave birth to her daughter right there in the house with her sister-in-law at her side. The sister-in-law helped clean up the baby and made her a delectable hot meal. For the first time in months, Jackie felt loved. She thanked the women as she held her daughter. She named the little girl, Beth, after her own mother.

Beth grew and became a beautiful little dark-haired child, very much resembling Jackie. For a reason that she couldn't understand, it bothered Jordan that Beth looked so much like her.

As he had told Beth all those months ago, he wanted nothing to do with the child and he stayed true to his word. Jordan ignored his daughter, never holding, feeding or playing with her. Having this baby girl did not bring Jackie happiness or bring about the change that she thought would happen.

When Beth was a year old, Jordan decided it was time for Jackie to be pregnant. So that is what immediately happened. Jordan told Jackie that he needed a boy this time and if she would simply give him a boy, he could be happy with her once again. His happiness was all up to her.

Happiness had eluded Jackie for so long that she too desperately wanted and prayed for a boy. She knew that making Jordan happy would bring about her own happiness too.

Nine months later, Joshua, a beautiful blond boy was born. He had his Father's nose and dimpled chin and as everyone in town told Jordan over and over, "Joshua is the spitting image of you." Jordan was the proud papa. He took Joshua everywhere with him, showing off his son to anyone that he met.

Almost overnight, Jordan became a new man. He travelled less so he could spend more time with his son and Jackie. He finally had become a satisfied man, husband and father. Jackie lost her weight quickly to please her husband and put herself back on birth control.

Jordan quickly regained his obsession with his lovely and beautiful wife again. Times were good. She had given him a son, and for that he was very pleased. With her husband's growing obsession for her, she was even more eager to please him, determined to be everything Jordan wanted. The three J's, as Jordan called them, were very happy, but Beth remained on the outside as the unwanted daughter. And now for the first time to her mother as well.

Life for Jackie kept improving with the birth of her son. One evening while Jordan was holding his year old son, he asked his wife to come and sit next to them, patting the sofa cushion beside him. He talked of her beauty and her wonderful job as baby Joshua's mother all the while kissing and caressing her face.

He told her how delighted he was that his son looked like him, and how proud he was of both Joshua and her. He told Jackie that he hoped that someday she would have another son to round out their beautiful family. She shook her head in agreement but also knew what Jordan meant. Beth was not, nor would ever be, a part of "them".

Jackie was intent on pleasing Jordan whatever the cost. Her obsession for his 'love' grew stronger every day. She had to have it, like the air she breathed. He loved Joshua and he loved her more than ever and she couldn't bear to lose that.

One sunny spring day, Jordan came home early from being out of town surprising Jackie by saying that they would be moving. He had bought a house on the "right side of the tracks", and it was time for his family to live the good life that they deserved.

That evening, he took her over to their beautiful new family home that he had purchased. The house was abuzz with activity. A large moving van was pulled up to the front doors and a little man, the decorator, was running around directing the movers as to where to place the new furniture. Jordan had seen to it that the house and everything in it was perfection.

After the tour of their new home, Jordan turned to his wife in the massive front hallway as they were leaving and told her that he loved her and Joshua more than anything else in his world and gave her a box from his pocket. When Jackie looked inside, she couldn't contain her excitement and jumped into Jordan's arms, kissing the man she loved with a passion. The beautiful diamond ring fit her perfectly, as she knew it would. The couple left the dream home hand in hand, happier than they had ever been before.

Within weeks, the couple and their children moved into their new home. Living in such a prestigious neighborhood pleased Jordan. He continually showered Jackie with lavish gifts so she would brag to the neighbors, making him look like the ever-perfect husband.

Jackie's life did seem perfect, except for one thing, her daughter. She had no doubt that Jordan adored her and their son; he made that perfectly clear. But he still ignored Beth and was constantly annoyed with her, punishing her for things that didn't matter. Beth was unhappy most of the time and started acting out in public to get his attention. Jackie knew that he demanded having the image of the 'perfect' family man. That seemed to be his newest obsession. He ran for councilman and overwhelming won. Everyone in town adored him and the upstanding citizen that he was.

Keeping up with 'The Jones' was important and necessary in their lives. Jackie jumped on that bandwagon with her husband and enjoyed the ride. Jordan's obsessions became her obsessions. She too, became very upset with Beth and her tantrums and inappropriate behavior in public.

So one spring day, without any hesitation in her mind, Jackie knew what she had to do. It would be her secret for now. When the right time came to tell Jordan her plan she knew he would be proud of what she would do and even prouder of her than he already was.

The next morning, harboring her feelings of purpose and love for her husband, Jackie gets up extra early to ready herself for the day. She pulls out a dirty pair of worn out jeans from the hamper as well as a soil-stained t-shirt that she had worn in the garden a couple of days before and puts them on. She finds her grimy pair of old tennis shoes that she only wears when in the garden and ties them onto her feet. Without brushing her beautiful dark hair, she gathers it into a high ponytail on top of her head. She wears no makeup at all.

Looking in the mirror, she smiles, satisfied with her appearance. Before leaving the house she picks up the copy of the Spartanburg Daily News, and writes down the information that she needs. Strapping Beth into her car seat, Jackie drives the two and a half hours to Spartanburg, West Virginia. She parks her car down the block from her destination and walks with her daughter on her hip to the front doors of the massive Gothic home.

Above the front doors of the home, Jackie cannot help but notice the grotesque gargoyles glaring at her with their beady eyes from their stone perch above. It is as if the little band of three demons is chastising her for wanting happiness. For a split second, she wonders if what she is doing is evil. The thought is fleeting as she thrusts it quickly out of her mind and tells herself, "Happiness is all I have ever wanted. Sacrificing my child is the means to that end."

With that, Jackie bursts through the doors in earnest, willing to seize her prize.

As she reaches to close the doors behind her, Jackie sees the diamond ring that Jordon had given her when they moved into their beautiful home; it is still on her finger. That mistake could cost her. She is not willing to let her happiness slip away so easily. With her back still to the desk, she tears a piece of her t-shirt off at the bottom and wraps the ring tightly in it.

An old nun looks up from the reception counter as she hears the ruckus at the front doors. Concerned, she scoots from around the counter to meet the lovely lady holding a child.

"Is everything all right? What can I help you with, Miss?"

Without hesitation, Jackie stuffs the fabric wrapped ring into her daughter's pants pocket to hide it. Plastering a concerned look on her face, she turns to face the woman. Using the accent she so frequently heard spoken around the small coal-mining town she lived in, she quietly says,

"I cannot keep my little girl. I have no money and I know she will have a better life being adopted by a nice wealthy family. I have to give her up."

The elderly nun looks at Beth, then at Jackie and says, "Please join me over here at the counter, Miss."

Jackie follows the nun back to the mahogany counter. With that spoken lie, Jackie forces a giant tear to fall from her eye, leaving her cheek and dramatically landing with a silent splash on the marble topped counter. The silence hangs eerily in the room while the matronly woman waits and hopes that the woman before her will change her mind.

Jackie stares straight ahead with no emotion. The grandmotherly nun reaches for the child with a look equally void of emotion, and takes the beautiful little girl from her mother.

"Oh," says Jackie, finally looking the woman in the eye as she hands her young daughter over to her, "Her name is Beth."

"And what is your name, Miss?"

"It is Jackie. That is all."

The nun pulls some papers out from under the counter in an attempt to get Jackie to sign them. Getting flustered, Jackie turns suddenly, not looking back at her daughter or the woman, and sprints out of the front doors eager to grab hold of all the love and happiness that is waiting her back home with Jordan.

Reaching her car quickly, a huge sigh of relief escapes from her lips. The cost of giving up the ring and her daughter is nothing compared to her hopes of future happiness. Just then the baby boy within her belly gives her a sharp kick. Jackie grabs her belly delighted to feel the new life inside her for the first time. Without hesitation, Jackie pushes the events of the day out of her mind as she races home towards her forever happiness.

Little Jacob weighing in at four pounds, two ounces is born on March 2nd in the beautiful new hospital where he is given the best of care. He arrives two months early so he must stay longer than the typical amount of time allotted for a newborn. His father stays at his infant son's bedside day and night. The only day the father leaves the hospital is the day of his wife's funeral. And the only time he takes his adoring eyes off his infant son is when he must write the obituary for his beloved wife.

> *Mrs. Jackie Smithy, loving mother and wife of prominent councilman, Mr. Jordan Smithy, never regained consciousness after a fiery head on collision on Highway 93 outside the town of Spartanburg on October 2. She remained in a coma due to severe head trauma and burns over half her body. She died shortly after she delivered their premature son, Jacob Jordan Smithy, on March 2nd. Mr. and Mrs. Smithy's daughter, Elizabeth Ann Smithy, died in the crash. Sadly, her remains could not be recovered.*
>
> *The memorial service and funeral for Mrs. Smithy and their daughter, Beth, will be held at Lawless Funeral Home on March 10 at 3:00 p.m.*

Wearing a somber face, devoid of expression, Jordan stands with his son at his wife's grave pleased at the size of the large crowd that had gathered to show their sympathy.

CHAPTER 6

The Orphanage

Beth continues riding along the tracks in silence looking out the train car window when a sweet but nosy woman sitting next to her on the train, asks Beth her name. Usually Beth won't engage in conversation with anyone, especially a stranger, but for some reason she decides to trust this woman, somehow feeling a connection with her.

Looking at the woman she answers, "My name is Beth."

"Oh, What a lovely name, dear. Is it short for Elizabeth?"

"No, it is just Beth, plain Beth."

"Well, Beth, tell me all about yourself." The woman smiles a toothless grin up at her.

Looking into the woman's eyes, Beth sees her loneliness. Loneliness is an emotion she recognizes. With pity and understanding taking over, Beth steps out of her comfort zone and decides to entertain her with her own story.

"Okay, sure." Beth takes a deep breath and begins. "I will begin my life's story with my mother." She pauses again allowing the words "my mother" to rest in her mouth for a moment.

She continues. "Jackie, the mother I don't remember, abandoned me at a very young age. The nuns told me that I was around three years old on the day my mother dropped me off at the orphanage. The nuns couldn't know for sure because my mother didn't leave a birth certificate or tell them my age or even my full name."

"So how old are you now, dear?" the woman interrupts.

"Twenty-three...I will be twenty three next month." Beth answers and continues with her life story.

"My mother left me at St. Cecelia's Convent on a beautiful October morning, so I am told. I know that fact because one of the nuns told me about that day when I was five years old and I have never forgotten it. The nun was furious with me for lying to her. I remember her exact words to me. *'I can see why your mother left you here at the orphanage, Beth. I would have left you too, if I were your mother! You are a terrible, very bad, little girl.'* That old, fat nun spanked my bottom and pushed me into the corner to sit and think about how very bad I obviously had been as a three year old and how bad I still was at five years old. I did as I was told and thought about the bad little girl that I was many times over for many years to come. From that moment on, I *was* that terrible little girl, just like that old nun told me I was."

The old woman interrupts Beth again, saying, "That is awful Beth. I am so sorry. I don't understand how some people can be so cruel."

Beth smiles sweetly at the old woman suddenly glad she is telling her story. Beth continues, "Not one of the nuns in the convent liked me or spent any time with me. I didn't mind though. I was a loner and liked it that way. I never once received hugs or loving pats like some of the other kids there did and no one ever seemed interested in adopting me.

Thinking back, it might have been because I wore a smile-less expression every day that I lived there. I couldn't smile because I hated it there. I hated my mother, and I hated everyone around me. I did practice smiling in the mirror at night when no one else was around, but I never allowed anyone to see it." Beth smiles as she allows herself this admission.

"I hated those nuns, I hated the orphanage and I hated most of the other kids, until I met Melody. Melody was bad sometimes, like me. She always seemed to be in one corner of the room while I was in the other. We made up a secret language that only the two of us knew so we could communicate to each other while we spent our time in the corners. That made our time sitting in the corner better.

Mostly, we communicated our hatred for the nuns saying that they were fat, ugly, stinky, and mean, and that they were a coven of witches.

When we were alone and could actually talk with real words, we started making up a story about the wicked witches of St. Cecelia's Convent."

Beth pauses, looking at her companion for affirmation.

"Go on dear," the woman shakes her head in agreement.

"I can remember every detail about our story even now. We laughed together saying that someday we would publish our story. And those old witchy nuns would get in trouble from the priest. That made us laugh every time so I guess I did smile with Melody, but she was the only one."

"Did you ever write your book about the nuns, dear?" Beth's new friend asks.

"Oh no, I never did...but maybe I will someday." Beth answers.

"You do have a lovely smile, Beth."

"Thank you."

At this point, the sweet lady grabs Beth's hand and pats it with her gloved hand. "I am still listening." The compassion in her voice encourages Beth to continue with her story.

"Melody and I planned to leave that place from the time we were about ten years old. We plotted and schemed our get-away plan for an entire year. She hated the nuns and the orphanage about as much as I did. My first friend, actually, my only friend and I became very close, giggling and laughing and never telling another soul about our plan. I loved Melody. Having a friend like her was something special to me and I probably would have lost my mind without her.

But when we were almost twelve, she disappeared. I am not exactly sure what happened. I think she may have gotten adopted. Before she disappeared, she had begun to change. She told me it was a change for the better and that she did not want to get into trouble anymore. She said she wanted to be a good girl because she wanted to get adopted more than anything. Finally, she told me that she would not run away with me. She thought that if she were a sweet girl, some nice family would want her."

Beth's eyes lose their focus as she begins thinking to herself about her friend. She realizes that she misses Melody.

Continuing she says, "As Melody got nicer, she tried to convince me that I shouldn't leave the orphanage. She would tell me that "out there" were bad people and scary things and that I was safer and better off in the orphanage with the nuns to protect me. When she talked like that, which seemed to happen much more often the older we got, I would get very angry and argue with her. I couldn't understand why she changed the way she felt. She told me that she was being the voice of reason for me.

The day Melody disappeared was the worst day of my life. She was not in her bed when I woke up. She was nowhere in the orphanage. I searched everywhere. I tried to ask all the nuns where she had gone. They never would give me a straight answer. They would look at one another and at me like they held a deep secret and shake their habit-covered heads at me like I could not be privy to their surreptitious information. My world crumbled then. I cried for the first time ever over another person. I missed my best friend so much and wanted her back. And I hated the wicked nuns even more.

With Melody's sudden absence, the thought of running away from that dreadful place took over my every thought. My plan was done, all I had left to do was put it into action."

"Have you ever seen Melody again, dear?" the sweet old lady asks.

"Oh yes, I have from time to time. She shows up and we talk. She is still my best friend to this day."

Beth continues her story.

"The plan to escape was a simple plan, actually. At supper one night, I got up from the orphan's table and made my way into the kitchen with my tray. That was normal enough.

The cooks and nuns were sitting on one end of a long table talking and eating together in the kitchen and did not notice me as I snuck past them. I simply slipped out the kitchen door unbeknownst to the wardens of the orphans. I made sure I didn't let the screen door slam behind me. It was dark and I ran far away. I ran until I could run no more. It was one of the scariest nights I have ever spent. By morning, I had made it to downtown and found an open dumpster behind a restaurant. There I found food that had been thrown out. Eating my fill, I realized that I had been successful. And that felt good.

I really don't think the nuns looked for me too hard. They were probably glad the troublemaker and "sad-sack" as they loved to call me, was gone. I know they received some sort of money for the number of children they took care of, and I am sure they missed my monetary equivalent. But, I also know, without a shadow of a doubt, they didn't miss me."

The sweet lady squeezes Beth's hand and tells her that she is so sorry about her awful mother and what she did to her all those many years ago. Beth hesitates and then shows her the ring on her hand, saying,

"My mother gave me this ring so I figure she wasn't all bad."

CHAPTER 7

Fireside Conversation

Sandy sits down the bottle of merlot on the dresser as pulls her well-worn jeans and a t-shirt out of her suitcase and begins to change her clothes. As she dresses, Sandy can't help but wonder if she and Andrew will pick up from where they left off so many long years ago. Smiling at herself in the mirror, she hopes so.

Sandy feels the rushing breeze pushing through the screen. It is cool. Closing the window, she puts on her extra warm wooly socks as she slides around the room looking for her brush. The windy ferry ride, and the breezy car ride, had had its way with her hair. The soft curls are long gone, leaving in their place a tangled and snarled mess. She does the best she can with her red hair, freshens her makeup and opens the bedroom door.

With a deep breath, not knowing what to expect from Andrew, Sandy anxiously pads down the hall with the bottle of wine in tow. He is chopping vegetables with his back to her across the room. Her padded feet skate along the slippery floor and she slides right into him. The two laugh for a brief moment as Sandy hands him the bottle of wine. He smiles his familiar smile at her.

"Can I help?" she questions. "Nope." he simply says. "Go, sit by the fire and warm up. It is chilly tonight."

On the other side of the room, a roaring fire is burning in the huge stone fireplace. Drawn to its warmth, Sandy heads towards it and watches the flames as they dance towards the ceiling.

"What a delightful spot." She shouts to Andrew as she puts her hands towards the flames and rubs them together to help warm them.

Framing the stone fireplace are shelves filled with many books. Studying the wall of his books, she sits down in a large chair facing the fire. The ocean view has disappeared from the window now, giving way to darkness. But, the beauty of it is still etched in her memory and Sandy longs to see it again.

Once again, Andrew pulls her from her thoughts as he is suddenly standing before her holding a glass of wine. As she reaches for the glass, and thanks him, tiredness begins to take over. It had been a long day of plane, taxi, car and ferry rides. He retreats to the kitchen again as Sandy leans back on the cushion of the chair, exhausted.

Pulling her long legs up to her chest, she feels the wine as it fills her mouth and wraps around her tongue. Swallowing slowly and sighing deeply, she tastes the cherry undertones of the smooth bodied merlot. She settles into the cozy chair waiting for the wine to warm and relax her. Quiet jazz fills the room and the absence of conversation isn't uncomfortable. It feels good and right. Something neither of them had felt in some time.

There is an antique table next to her chair with a beautiful handmade pottery lamp sitting on it. Sandy admires the amber stained glass shade, which gives off a soft glow matching her mood. On the other side of the table is another chair exactly like the one she sits in. Soon, Andrew joins her there.

With an effortless feeling of comfort, he places a big salad and two bowls on the table and refills her wine glass, leaving a fresh bottle on the table beside them. The salad is delicious and quite filling. The homegrown lettuce is topped with feta cheese, fresh tomatoes and herbs and homemade vinaigrette. They talk of family and work, and other mundane topics.

Thinking that the salad is all she needs until morning, she is surprised when he gets up, gathers their bowls and brings out another bowl of pasta with shallots, mushrooms, and chicken scattered throughout. The whole dish is topped with a creamy white wine sauce. Even though Sandy thinks she couldn't possibly eat another bite, she devours all the gourmet pasta he scoops into her fresh bowl.

As the evening continues to unfold, the wine relaxes both of them. They talk late into the evening of their old college days, laughing and telling more stories than either of them knew that they remembered. Sandy laughs about what a womanizer Andrew was back in the day.

He laughs along with her saying, "But I was young and stupid back then. Maybe I have just grown up a little. I hope that I have. Really, I think that I have."

"Well, I sure hope so!" Sandy laughs. "And I am still the sweet red haired girl I always was in college."

For some reason, perhaps because he had had too much wine at this point, Andrew brings up his best friend saying, "I sure do miss Jim. I wish he were here with us right now, talking about the good ole days. Boy would he have stories to tell on me."

Sandy is suddenly silent and Andrew looks over at her and sees that she is staring into the fire with tears in her eyes.

"I am so sorry, Sandy. I shouldn't have mentioned Jim." Feeling awkward and mad at himself for ruining the mood, he reaches for her hand. "Please forgive me."

As Sandy gets up, she smiles softly down at him, "It is okay, Andrew. I miss him too."

She brushes his face with her hand. He stands up as she wraps her arms around him. Suddenly feeling the need of comfort as well as the feel of her body next to his, Andrew returns her hug with gentleness and warmth that lingers longer than expected. His fingers brush her bangs and travel around her cheeks to her lips, as they look lovingly into each other's eyes, both desperate for more.

Whether out of some left over guilt she feels from long ago or because she doesn't want to move too quickly, she hears herself whisper to him, "I must go to sleep now. Good night, Andrew."

Simultaneously they both realize that it had been a perfect night, in a perfect place and they would and should leave it at that. Andrew smiles sweetly at her. Neither wanting it, but both of them finding it appropriate for the night to end.

"Good night, Sandy."

Before sitting back down in front of the fire, Andrew pours another glass of wine and goes over to the bookcases and pulls out a journal he had left under a stack of magazines. He starts flipping the pages of the book, finding himself at the worn pages that he has read over so many times. He thinks back to his first encounter with his therapist.

CHAPTER 8

Andrew's Journal

"I am just not a journaling kind-of-guy. I just don't spend that much time working through my feelings, or whatever you call it, Doc, and I surely don't want to spend the time trying to write them down."

"Then, why are you here?" spoke Dr. Bashier with a blank stare.

…And he had a point. I did not want to delve into my thoughts, but as a result my thoughts were revolting against me. After Jim's death, I had started having trouble going to sleep at night. Then, I was staying awake all night. My life had never been one of introspection, but it seems as if that was changing.

"OK Doc", Andrew finally admits, "if you think it will help…and I am not saying that it will, but I will give it a try. So, I am supposed to write a book?"

"Andrew…just put your feelings down on paper. Whenever you can't sleep, or whenever you are feeling sad, just write down the first thoughts that come to your mind. Then, think about what you wrote and why you might have written it. It's just a simple exercise. Don't over think it."

That conversation took place four years ago and it was the last time he saw or talked to Dr. Bashier. Taking another sip from his glass, Andrew wishes that he had let him know how much that exercise had played a part in him finding himself again.

Sitting comfortably on his couch with Toby at his feet, Andrew continues to flip the pages of his worn journal, realizing that it has been a long time since his last entry. Having read over his notes many times before, he understands how the words were so close to his heart back then…just as his old leather journal is now. Finding the section about Jim, Andrew slowly reads his entries.

Tuesday, October 4

Jim…best friend. Oldest friend. He was certainly a longhaired hippie type if I ever knew one. He was not always the kind of guy your parents wanted you to hang around with, but with enough time, even parents grew to like him. He was always too loud, too big, too obnoxious, too kind, too caring, and I loved him. I never had a brother, but I could not imagine loving a brother more that I loved Jim.

Everyone was always laughing when they were around him. It was not that he was so funny, but he made you believe that wherever you were with him, you were in the best place possible. It seems a contradiction, but he was a giant pixie…a magical entity in a troll's body.

Friday October 7

Sandy…my second best friend. The closest thing I had to a sister. My best friend's girl friend. My best friend's wife. The source of so much guilt.

I met Sandy my freshman year of college. She was eighteen and I was twenty-one. She used to tell me that growing up, she was always tall and lanky. Her hair was too red, her teeth were too big, and her body was too thin. However, you could tell that she was becoming a beautiful woman that first year in college, but she still saw herself as that fifteen-year old gangly girl. Part of her beauty came from that… the fact that she was a very confident and self-assured "fifteen year old".

She was the girl that I could always talk to. We talked about girls, who I should date, who I should not date. She even suggested girls that she thought I might get lucky with…and I dated them all. She would say to me, "Just go on a date, a single date, with the poor girl. Don't get involved. You will just break her heart." I always argued with her, but I knew that she was right. And now years later to my adult shame, I realize I did not treat most of those girls well.

Note to self: OK, Dr. Bashier…I get it. If I had been honest with myself, I was always crazy about Sandy. It was just easier being her friend than taking a chance with her and screwing it up. I was always afraid to entertain the idea that she was more to me than a friend. Even over the next couple of years as she grew out of her adolescence and became comfortable in her new body, I refused to acknowledge any feeling for her other than friendship.

I think that is enough for tonight, Doc.

Monday, October 20

Me…Stupid, self-absorbed, too busy chasing every skirt that passed by my peripheral vision. That about covers it. Thinking that one-night stands were a "life plan" for my immediate future, I introduced my two best friends and set them up on their first date…and to no one's surprise, they hit it off beautifully. And why shouldn't they; they were both amazing. Their individual attributes just seemed to complete each other's. Her hands were so small, and Jim's so big that his hand would completely envelope hers. I always noticed when they held hands because her hands would disappear into his. They dated and didn't stop until they married. It was three years I think.

When Sandy and Jim got married, I was his best man. To say it was bittersweet is pretty much an understatement, but I was sad when the two drove off together after the wedding. I knew I would miss my two best friends, and I knew it would never be the same because they had each other now.

Sandy and Jim never had any children. I don't know why. Maybe because, they weren't a good physical match…with him being so big and she being so small. (I always imagined a St. Bernard trying to mate with a French Poodle. That is a little analogy that I choose to never share with them.) Their lack of children never seemed to matter to them though. Their lives were full and happy.

They moved to Dallas after college, and I would visit them when I could. One day Jim tried to explain to me that Sandy was his best friend…and the love of his life. He said that he hoped I would meet someone someday that would be that for me. I appreciated the thought, but I was just not ready for that kind of relationship.

As the next few years went by, Sandy grew into an extraordinary woman. It was becoming harder and harder for me to view her as my sister. Her long, wavy, thick hair; beautiful smile; wide eyes; and long legs turned heads. When she walked into a room, she commanded the attention of every person there. And the best part was that she still didn't know just how gorgeous she was. Somehow, she retained the ability to not acknowledge her own beauty, and to focus on others and their needs interests and talents.

Wednesday, November 7

I don't remember the exact date, but I moved to Nashville shortly after Jim and Sandy were married. I like to think that I was ready for a serious relationship, but there were a lot of single and slightly married women out there. I had my choice of make believe cowgirls and country singers that were strong on looks and weak on everything else. However, you can only wake up so many nights in a different apartment wondering where you are before you start to want something more.

At least that's what I told Sandy one day while we were talking on the phone. I had called to talk to Jim, but he wasn't home when I called. Sandy talked to me for an hour that day catching me up with their life. She chitchatted about work, their house, friends, and family...basically whatever popped into her head. I listened. I grew to enjoy talking to her on the phone, and we did it fairly often. She was always happy and cheered me up, and I began to listen to her advice on women.

Sunday, November 18

Well Doc...(Where ever you may be)...I guess it was about two years ago next week that Jim and Sandy invited me for Thanksgiving Dinner. This particular Thanksgiving was a cold one in Dallas. We were trying to deep-fry a turkey outside on the patio while simultaneously trying not to burn down their house. It was pretty funny, really. We would run outside to check on it, and then run back in before the cold air numbed our hands. Jim was basically in charge of the frying, and Sandy and I were preparing everything else in the kitchen.

Sandy and I had picked up the pace as we were cooking, and I was reaching across her to grab a tomato for the salad, when my hand brushed against her breast. We both stopped and looked at each other. She immediately blushed a dark red, but I could not read the look on her face beneath the blush. Without a word, I leaned over and kissed her lips deeply. Both of us were surprised and turned aside to continue our work. I have no idea why I kissed her then except that it was something I had wanted to do for a long time.

So Doc... Here in lies the basis of my guilt. I know that a stolen kiss, does not make me a mass murderer, but it was not *just* a kiss. I have replayed that kiss in my mind a thousand times, and each time I remember the smell of the kitchen, the smell of her hair, the taste of her lips. And every time I think about the kiss, I think about the pain I would have caused Jim if he had known.

Doc, I don't remember the author, but someone once wrote about a kiss that all future kisses would be measured against and found lacking. For me, kissing Sandy in front of her sink, with her husband, my best friend outside, was *that kiss*. It was adultery in every sense of the word but one.

The weekend was over and I went home.

Tuesday, December 7

I was invited back to their house for Christmas four weeks later. I do not know if it was Jim or Sandy's idea. I had not been able to get "that night in front of the sink" out of my mind, but I had made up my mind that nothing else would happen...ever.

When I arrived at their front door on Christmas Eve, it was late. I didn't plan to be so late but my car had been acting up and I had to stop and have it looked at a service station. The mechanic ended up replacing the alternator belt. I think it was 11:30 or later when I pulled in to their driveway.

Sandy met me at the door before I could ring the bell. Jim was already asleep. She opened the door and gave me her usual big hug and smile, saying "Merry Christmas!" I had my bag in my hand so I could only give her a one handed sister-hug. I put my bag down and said, "Now let's do this right." We hugged a second time, and I kissed her forehead. My lips lingered and she looked deep into my eyes. I didn't want to pull away from my best friend's wife, but I did.

We sat and talked in front of the Christmas tree lights and decaying embers of the night's fire. We sat knee to knee on the couch, and started telling stories about each other's Christmases past. She would giggle out loud from time to time, and I would yell "Hush!" laughing about Jim being asleep in the next room.

Unselfconsciously, she would touch my leg to make a point, or to swat at me for making a bad joke. There was an abrupt break in the conversation, and we both realized I was holding both of her hands in mine. I leaned in and with a kiss started the progression that effectively ended a long friendship. I will regret that night for the rest of my life. It was also the most incredible night of my life.

So Doc...How does a small town boy from Spring Hill, Tennessee reconcile making love to his best friend's wife outside their bedroom door on Christmas Eve...and then having to live with the fact that I would never see him again?

Doc...I don't even know if I could have faced him again.

But I never got the chance to see Jim again after that visit. I never even got the chance to make that decision. He was coming home from his office one rainy evening on the Dallas toll way when a van slid into his car, spinning him around and headlong into the guardrails on the side of the road. He died on the road alone with no one with him.

I flew in for his funeral and did not and could not look at Sandy. She hugged me when I first saw her, before the funeral, but that was it. Her eyes and mine did not meet. For both of us, it was very much on purpose.

I left Dallas and Jim's funeral with a deep, dark hole in my heart. I tried calling Sandy several times over the next few months, but she never answered. I knew in what was left of my heart that she couldn't bear the thought of seeing me again.

She moved back to Tennessee and near her folks. I am sure she was hoping to mend her guilty and broken heart. I lost contact with her.

...And so, I head into a new year *without* my two best friends... without *any* friends.

Putting the journal back in its spot under the magazines, Andrew sits for a good long while thinking about Jim. If it hadn't been for his weekly visits to his therapist during those years after Jim's death and the writing of these words, he wouldn't have been able to decipher the crippled beatings of his fragile and broken heart.

Flipping off the lights, he retreats to his bedroom with Toby leading the way.

CHAPTER 9

Remembering Beth

Bright light from the morning sun splashes into Sandy's window beckoning her to open her eyes and get up. The smell of the salty air and the sound of the loons loudly squawking through her slightly opened window serves as her "nature" alarm clock.

The biting breeze billows the curtains as they reach over to her. The tassels at the bottom edge of the curtains touch her bare shoulder like small fingers. Pulling the comforter tighter around her body, Sandy fights the urge to open her eyes. Too much wine from the night before and an ache in her head demands more sleep. For a moment, she wonders where she is, not able to remember. Andrew's face appears out of nowhere in her mind and a quick smile moves her face.

In the room across the hall, Andrew lies awake in his bed thinking of Sandy. His thoughts of her meander around in his mind aimlessly. A smile that he can't control slides across his face. How strange yet wonderful it is to have her here in my favorite place, he thinks as he replays the events of yesterday in his mind. Sandy still possesses that childlike sparkle in her eyes, eager to see and learn about everything around her and I love that. Andrew sighs.

His thoughts and smile continue. She had surprised me yesterday as I waited for her on the knoll at the ferry. I had looked down for a moment and when I looked up she was just there. Hoping to spot her first from my vantage point on the hill, I longed to take in her beauty at my leisure, before we actually met. But that was not meant to be. I looked up to see her curly red hair flying with the wind around her broad smiling face.

She came towards me as she bounced out of her car and all I knew to do was hug her. But it was too quick and too hard; I knew that the minute I did it. I had a few minutes to gather myself as we drove along the road separately before we got to my cottage. I was thankful for that.

I wonder how the week will go. Will it be awkward or comfortable? If last night is any indication, I think we will be relaxed and enjoy each other's company. I know one thing for sure I will not mention Jim again. I hated to see her cry last night. We rarely have been alone in the past so perhaps we should go slowly, very slowly.

Andrew thought of her face and how she wore her wrinkles well. She had thin arms under the soft brown sweater she had on yesterday and he couldn't help but notice her long legs as they seductively crept from below her skirt as she got out of her car. She definitely didn't show signs of her age.

Most importantly, he loved the fact that Sandy was awe struck with the view when they finally reached the cottage. He had hoped it would have that affect on her. It was a small thing, but this cottage sitting on the high banks of the wild sea as well as his life here, characterizes who he is now. He hoped Sandy would see that.

To bring his home into focus for Sandy, Andrew had arranged for Corbin to give them the "Grand Tour" as he called it around the island in his boat. Corbin was a good friend and knew the history of this place like the back of his hand. Andrew knew that his smaller boat wouldn't be nearly as comfortable as Corbin's boat and besides Corbin rides these waters every day. Sandy would like him and he would like her.

As Andrew thinks about the day ahead, Toby stirs, wakes up, and jumps onto his bed. "Are you ready to go out, big 'un?"

"Okay, I take that look as a yes, but we have to be quiet. Sandy is still in her room sleeping. I think we have plenty of time to walk this morning before she wakes."

Andrew pulls on his trousers and an old sweatshirt; grabs his cap and shoes and heads to the kitchen to start the coffeemaker. Once done, he and Toby head out the front door for their morning walk.

The trees hang easily over the road bending their boughs ever so slightly reaching towards the earth and then springing back en route for the open sky as the wind teases. The birds are up and chirping loudly inviting Toby to play. He accepts their invitation as he does every morning, and runs into the woods chasing their birdcalls. Reappearing beside Andrew, he darts off in a different direction, skirting the edge of the woods. It is a game he loves to play. He loves their morning walks as much as Andrew does.

Andrew tries to keep his thoughts from remembering, especially today, but like always, the memories creep back as if an unwanted cat, invading his peaceful new life.

Beth…He tosses her name around his mind, playing with the memories once again.

He knows Beth would have liked it here too, sometimes he wishes he had found this tiny island before…before she left him, or did he leave her? Time had healed some of the pain, but mornings always brought out the demons…the heartache once again.

Andrew loved to remember their life together before…before all hell broke loose. They were happy and so in love. He knew even today, many years later as he walked in the morning sunlight, that part of him still loved Beth. He simply couldn't release her from his heart. Her long dark hair and smiling lips slipped back into his mind's eye as it did every morning on his walk with Toby.

Her smile had stolen his heart many years before and even now stole his thoughts for a moment, for just a moment, as he thought of her before; before the adoption, when his whole heart was hers.

He stopped walking, lost in his thoughts of Beth. She was absolutely the most beautiful woman he had ever seen. Everyone said they made the perfect pair. Remembering the day they met, Andrew walks on down the road again, recreating the scene in his mind. He sees himself walking into the snack room on the second floor in his office building in downtown Nashville. He was very busy that day and he needed a 'pick me up'. The project that Carl had given him was a big one and would take him all day. He knew then that he would be lucky if he had it done when Carl had to go to the meeting at six o'clock that evening.

The snack room did not carry his normal fare, especially the coffee. But Starbucks was around the block and he did not have the time to walk all the way there. He would have to make due with vending machine coffee. He remembered scanning the room to see if anyone he knew was taking a break. Joe, his buddy from the office, was sitting at a nearby table. Grabbing his coffee out of the machine, he goes to sit with Joe.

The two start up a short conversation.

"Hey Joe, what's going on?"

"Not much, Andrew, taking a break. What about you, man?"

"Oh I've been working on that project Carl wants done. I needed some coffee. This is the fastest option."

Then Andrew remembers taking a big swig of the hot coffee. It was awful.

"This coffee tastes like sewer water!" and he gets up to throw the full cup of coffee away.

That is when he sees her. She sits at the table by the window. The light streaming in casts a beam of sunlight onto her face. He thinks he has seen her before but he can't be sure. Where? She looks so familiar. Was it here in the snack room or somewhere else? She is perfect.

Joe interrupts his thoughts as he yells to him that he is heading back upstairs and that he would see him later.

"Yeah, see you later, Joe." Andrew yells back across the room.

His eyes turn back to the girl by the window to see her looking up from her phone. As she raises her chin, he sees her green eyes. She pulls her hair band from her hair allowing her black mane to fall below her shoulders and around her elbows. As she shakes her head, her long silky black hair shifts around in the sunlight giving it a sheen that grabs his attention.

She wears a bright green sleeveless silk tank top and a black skirt. She has long legs. A jacket hangs from the back of her chair. She nibbles at her sandwich pulling little pieces of the top slice of bread off and popping them slowly into her mouth with her fingers. Then she looks in Andrew's direction. He averts his eyes to the vending machine in an effort to cover his obvious stare. He puts money into the machine and pushes the button for a cheese burrito. He catches a glimpse of those beautiful green eyes again. They are like cat eyes. And they are so familiar.

She looks past him to the clock on the wall above the door. Her black eye makeup enhances the starkness of the green color. Does he know her? If so, he can't place where he has met her.

Then he grabs a napkin from the counter and takes his burrito over to the microwave. He places it inside pushing the one-minute button. He turns once again to see her getting out of her chair. She is tall.

She walks slowly to the water cooler and fills her cup with water, never looking up from her phone. He watches her as his burrito cooks. She is stunningly beautiful and he decides that he will have to talk to her. Taking his burrito from the microwave, he walks towards her table.

"Hello, I am Andrew. May I sit down?" he says to her.

The green-eyed beauty looks up from her phone and smiles. She has dimples in her cheeks but her vivid green eyes are what capture his soul, teasing his heart.

"Yes, of course. I will be leaving in a minute; you can have my table," she answers matter of factly.

He remembers being panicked that she didn't understand what he meant and quickly says, "Oh no, I was wondering if I could join you?"

"Of course, I am Beth." She shakes his hand as he sits down.

"Hi Beth. Have we met before?" he asks knowing that if they had, he most certainly would have remembered.

"I don't think so. I just moved here a month ago."

"Do you work in the building? Oh, and I am Andrew by the way."

"Yes, you told me you are Andrew." She giggles and her eyes dance as she continues, "I work on the sixth floor. I am the receptionist for Walker, Walker and Walker Attorneys. What about you?"

"I work for Hughes and Flannigan Inc. on the seventeenth floor."

They sit quietly for a few minutes and then Beth says, "Well, very nice to meet you Andrew, I really must go or I will be late, and Mr. Walker won't be happy with me, neither will the two other Mr. Walkers." She laughs again and stands up grabbing and putting on her jacket.

He stands up also and says, "I hope to see you again here." And he really meant it.

"Perhaps, I am here most days at 11:30 for lunch. Nice to meet you, Andrew."

She turns away from the table and walks over to the trashcan. He continues to watch her as she throws away her barely eaten sandwich, then turns to him and smiles. With that smile, Andrew fell hard. And with that smile began a love affair that he cannot forget no matter how hard he tries.

Realizing that he had been on his walk with Toby longer than he intended, he pulls himself back to this forgiving place he calls home. As he turns around to go home, the vivid green eyes of Beth turn to blue, as Sandy's face appears in his mind. Throwing his thoughts of Beth away, back into the small piece of his heart dedicated to her, Toby comes up beside him, and tilts his head.

"I'm alright Tobe - not to worry. I just had one of my moments. I'll be fine. We best be gettin' back. The coffee will be ready and Sandy will be awake soon." Andrew and Toby race each other to the cottage door. Toby leads the way, as he always does.

CHAPTER 10

Like a Baby

Sandy sits up in bed to listen. She hears the pulsating sounds of the surf beating the rocks below the cottage like an anxious drummer beating his drum with a rhythm only he can understand. The voices of the seagulls try their best to compete. The discord is both unsettling and calming at the same time.

She wraps her quilt tighter around her shoulders as she takes in all that is surrounding her. Mixed in amongst the ocean smells, there is coffee. The smell wanders into her nose making her dry mouth slightly water...the smell turning into a full-blown craving. Not only for the coffee taste, but also primarily because last night's wine had made her mouth dry.

Sandy slips her feet from under the comforter but just as quickly pulls them back, as the air is much too chilly for bare feet on a cold wooden floor. Scooping her socks from the floor, she puts them on as she looks to the fireplace, noticing there are no embers glowing. She doesn't have a bathrobe so she grabs the warm comforter. She pulls it off the bed, and wraps it around herself.

Running her fingers through her bed-head hair she moseys on into the kitchen. She finds Andrew all dressed and sitting by the fire reading a book, his coffee on the end table next to him. She makes a quick stop at the coffee maker to pick up a waiting mug and fills it with coffee. As she opens the refrigerator to get the creamer, he looks up from what he is reading, and motions for her to join him.

"How did you sleep?" he questions.

"Like a baby," she answers from the kitchen.

Andrew puts down his novel and pats the couch next to him as she enters the living room. The windows are all open and the stiff sea breeze fills the room. It is quite cool in a refreshing sort of way.

Are you up for a swim today? Or would you prefer a boat ride around the island? I am game for whatever you like." He offers with a smile.

Sandy didn't have to think for long, knowing that the water would be way too cold for this southern girl, so she quickly answers him, "Oh, a boat ride would be delightful."

"A boat ride it is then." He agrees.

Together they cuddle up on the couch enjoying the fire whilst sipping their coffee, without saying another word. Soon, Andrew gets up pulling Sandy with him and the two venture out onto the back porch. With their cups held closely to their chests, they stand together looking towards the sea. The stiff breeze blows somewhat harder out on the porch and Sandy must cuddle up tighter in the warmth of the comforter.

There, lying before her is the entire Atlantic Ocean. Not a speck of land is in sight. The sea is exhilarating to watch as it tumbles down onto the rocks. Sandy is mesmerized by its raw energy and beauty. Large boulders and smaller rocks, in different shades of gray litter the seashore. Time, wind and water have shaped them into perfection. Pine trees line the rocky shore. A lighthouse stands further down as if a sentry guarding the Maine coast against the sea.

An old whitewashed swing hangs from the roof on one end of the chipping and peeling porch, and dilapidated stairs leading down to the shore on the other. Andrew points out to Sandy that it is high tide now, which allows the water to forcefully lap the shore as well as the bottom of the cottage steps making walking and exploring the beach an impossibility. Beach combing is best done during low tide, he says.

"Okay, Captain, Yes, sir, I will remember those words of wisdom." She salutes Andrew smiling at him with an impish grin and scurries into the cottage for another cup of coffee and to get dressed.

After dressing, Sandy explores the other end of the cottage. There is another bedroom, and a large bath with a separate shower and freestanding tub. The second bedroom is much larger than the one she occupies. It has its own attached sitting area. Leather furniture and heavy plaid draperies hang from the windows there. This masculine looking bedroom with its heavy wood bed, nightstands and large dresser takes up the entire end of the hall, taking in views of the pine trees to the front and ocean in the back. This room has quite a stunning panoramic view.

After her self-guided tour of the cottage, she follows her nose into the big room again. She is led by the smell of bacon and eggs cooking on the stove. Her stomach begins to rumble. She didn't realize how hungry she was.

Andrew carries the food over to the long harvest table and pulls out a chair for her. After refilling their coffees, he pulls out the chair next to her and sits down. She begins to fill her plate. He laughs as her plate is piled high with eggs, toast, and bacon. He had forgotten how much she likes to eat. Luckily for Sandy, her body's metabolism is still high and her tiny frame can handle it. Their time together in Owl's Nest had begun and they both look forward with eager anticipation to their day together.

CHAPTER 11

The Grand Tour

Captain Corbin Adcock was one of the best boat captains, if not *the very best* boat captain, in all of Owl's Nest, as well as the surrounding waters including the many inlets around the neighboring islands and the mainland as well. And he knew it. After all, he had skippered many boats of many sizes over the past thirty years. He had spent most of his life on the water being the skipper of a large lobster boat. This smaller boat was one of his favorites and the easiest to navigate.

Adcock didn't particularly like the morning skies as he readied his boat for the day's excursion. Andrew had called him several days before to ask for a daylong boat trip around the island for him and his friend from the city. Not only was Andrew a friend but also a well-respected member of the community. Corbin was happy to oblige. And besides Andrew was paying him well.

To the untrained eye, the day seemed to be a beautiful one with blue skies and high cumulus clouds. But Corbin knew better. The water was choppy. Choppy waters can turn into stormy waters in a matter of minutes if the wind picks up. And *that* he didn't like. He knew he would have to pay close attention to the skies today.

The wind was coming out of the northeast and he didn't like nor'easters either. They were unpredictable. Corbin had a good boat, a sturdy boat, and he was proud of it as well as his ability to navigate it. The most recent weather report for the morning was good, so he put his nagging worries aside for the moment and continued making ready for the day.

When Andrew had approached Sandy that morning out on the porch with the idea of taking a boat ride around the island, she hesitated for a minute. On one hand, it would be great to see the island from the water, Sandy thinks, pulling into the various harbors around the island, but on the other hand, she knew far too well her fears of water. It had been years since that terrible day at the lake. She hadn't thought of that day in a long time. And she didn't want to. Thankfully, that day had almost been erased from her memory.

Sandy didn't want to come across as a scaredy cat to Andrew. And besides, he seemed excited about the boat trip and proud to share his little island with her, so she made the difficult decision to put on her big girl panties that morning and suck up her fear.

As she goes back to her room, she looks out the window and sees that her first full day on the island with Andrew appears to be a sunny and bright one. The waters look to be calm so Sandy focuses on her attire for a boat ride.

Pulling her khaki shorts out of her suitcase, she slips them on looking at her reflection in the dresser's mirror. They are a little shorter than she normally wears, but why have good legs if you don't show them off occasionally, she thinks. Yes, the shorts are perfect and make her look younger than her thirty-eight years.

Her long sleeved striped navy and white shirt screams boating and water; perfect for the day's activity. She had brought her wide-brimmed straw hat with her for just such and occasion. She slips it on her head hiding most of her red hair. Her boat shoes make her outfit complete. Taking one last glance in the mirror, she smiles at her reflection and is satisfied that Andrew will like what he sees.

Andrew is taken aback when Sandy walks into the kitchen where he is gathering drinks to bring along with them. She is gorgeous. Grabbing his jacket and his favorite Yankees baseball cap from the hall tree, he heads out the cottage door proud to be with her.

He notes the sky and the choppy water as he glances below to the ocean behind the cottage. Knowing how fast the weather changes on the sea, he is not as comfortable as he would have liked to be about their excursion. But then again, he is confident that Corbin wouldn't attempt to leave the dock if there was any question of their safety. Sandy's voice possessed the power to dissipate his worries as they make their way along the pitted road to the harbor.

Walking along the pier with a cooler of drinks and a most grateful heart, Andrew greets the fishermen as they head towards their homes after a long night out on the water. It is going to be a good day. Andrew feels it in his bones; this is going to be a day of fun and forever memories with a woman he longs to be with.

Corbin allows Andrew to introduce him to Sandy as the "best damn Captain in all of Maine". She shakes his hand and says, "I am glad to meet you and so glad that you are the BEST."

Sandy boards the boat after taking Corbin's extended hand. Before Corbin can say a word to her about the life jacket, she quickly puts it on as she sits. If the boat chair had had a seat belt, she would have worn that as well.

The two men look at each other and shrug their raised eyebrows as if to say, "Well, she knows her way around a boat, sort of."

There Sandy sits not looking at all comfortable, clinging to her colorful oversized bag that she has placed in her lap, which is overshadowing the rest of her tiny body. Her long, lanky legs dangle from the tall fishing chair.

She wears the too-large orange vest pulled tightly across her chest, and a ridiculously large straw hat sits awkwardly atop her strawberry curls hiding most of her face and hair. She looks quite comical and both men desperately try not to smile. She doesn't look at the men, only out towards the sea.

Staring at her for another minute, and noticing that she does not look in the least bit sexy, except for maybe her long youthful legs, Andrew feels a slight surge in his heart like an extra heartbeat. Turning his eyes from her, he quickly dismisses the feeling, and takes up a detailed conversation with Corbin about his boat.

As the three sailors make their way along the natural channel that surrounds the small island, Sandy notes all the cottages and larger homes dotting the seashore. Many of them have docks and a small boat or two tied tightly to the pier. The larger boats are anchored out in the small bays reclining lightly on the undulating waves.

When they round the bend, Corbin backs the engines down and they slowly enter a large harbor. This harbor is different from the one the ferry had docked at yesterday. It seems to be home to a fleet of fishing boats...lobster boats actually. They are painted in various colors and most of them whose lines were tied correctly bob up and down comfortably. Captain Adcock points out a certain boat in the group to Andrew. Sandy assumes he was talking to Andrew about his lobster boat.

Once they pull all the way into the harbor, the ocean calms significantly and Sandy begins to relax her hands that have been tightly gripping her bag. The sight before her is breathtaking and she soon forgets her fears, putting them away for now.

Andrew planned to take Sandy ashore here to visit the few shops that were along the pier. He had arranged with Corbin to drop them off for an hour to explore. He knows Sandy will enjoy poking along the streets seeing what the islanders have for sale.

As Captain Adcock pulls slowly up to the pier and ties off the boat, Sandy and Andrew disembark for their hour of shopping. It seems that this spot is popular with the tourists as many of them leisurely stroll in and out of the shops carrying packages and enjoying the cool August morning.

Andrew helps Sandy off the boat as she steps up and onto the pier. He cannot help but notice once again her long, tanned legs as she climbs upward onto the dock. He is amazed that she is even more beautiful than in years past.

He almost laughs out loud watching her maneuver her hat, whatnot bag, and his extended hand. Her appearance is very "put together" except for one thing: her curly, disheveled, and unruly dab of orange hair that peeks out from under her humongous hat. Her orange curls provide just the right amount of messiness and craziness needed to make her outward appearance just to the left of perfect. And he realizes that is what he likes best about her.

Sandy releases her hold of Andrew's hand when she is up on the dock, although he wishes she hadn't. They stroll together along the dock slowly, watching the fishermen putting away their gear and nets as they secure the lobster pots onto the decks for their next run.

Sandy can see that the lobstermen are a rough and rugged bunch, each with their own hard life etched upon their faces - lives lived on the sea, making each wrinkle more prominent and seemingly count for more. Some of them smile and nod as the couple make their way along the pier to the shore, but most are too busy or tired to even notice them.

Climbing the metal ramp between the dock and the shore, Sandy can't help but notice how absolutely perfect her surroundings are. If she could paint a picture of life on an island off the coast of Maine, this is exactly what she would sketch. The row of colorful buildings sits along the serpentine road that hugs the rocky shore. It is breathtaking and predictable all at the same time.

People smiling, carrying colorful bags and wearing just as colorful jackets make the scene one from a Norman Rockwell painting. Several islanders sit on the benches that litter the sidewalk. She knows they must be 'Mainers' because they sit so comfortably as if they had no plans to move anytime soon. These locals appear more rugged and worn than the tourists. They are a group with character. This is their home; they are comfortable here and they dream of none other.

The tourists seem to go about their business feeling lucky to be here for a time; and at least for a while, suppressing thoughts of their jobs, homes, and busy lives elsewhere. Corralling her thoughts back, she focuses on the handsome man next to her. She notices right away that he nods to most of the men - the ones on the benches. With their nods to one another, they seem to say so much more than words ever could convey in the city. This unspoken language is all around her, but she is not privileged to know it.

As she and Andrew approach the first little shop, he opens the door and puts his hand on Sandy's back guiding her into the shop. He can feel the small curve of her back and so wishes he can leave his hand there. But she moves on through the door and reaches for a small wooden statue of a fisherman, content now to be shopping.

As they proceed leisurely from one shop to the next, Andrew keeps up his silent and secret conversations with the locals. However, Sandy realizes that their long stares and their knowing looks express approval to Andrew.

She enjoys their excursion more for Andrew's company than the shops. And Sandy does love to shop. It is a pleasant and relaxing way to spend an hour. As the time passes, her bag grows heavier and heavier with the added weight of each trinket she purchases along the way. She is pleased when Andrew offers to carry it for her, putting the canvas handles over his shoulder leaving his hand free to hold hers. As their shopping time disappears, so does the sun. The warmth from the sun wanes quickly as it hides behind the multiplying cumulus clouds.

Sandy pulls her sleeves down wishing she had worn her jeans instead of shorts today. They talk of the shops, the town, and her souvenirs as they make their way back to the boat. Andrew is being attentive to their conversation, but he is also quite aware of the growing height of the clouds that continue to build skyward as they walk.

Corbin is waiting for them on the dock as they approach the boat.

"It has gotten quite cloudy." Sandy says nervously to Corbin as she peers above her head and descends from the dock into the waiting boat. Corbin looks up too forcing an unbothered look to appear on his face.

As the small boat makes its way slowly through the anchored fishing boats, the couple cuddles up together on the bench seat in the rear. It had gotten much cooler now that the sun hides behind the clouds and the wind in turn takes its cue from them.

Sandy shivers from the cold, but mostly from the fear that is slowly building inside her. Seeing her shake, Andrew puts his arm tightly around her shoulders. She pushes against his body to shield herself from the weather and from her fears.

Corbin knows the situation on the water is worsening, but he doesn't want to alarm his passengers or cut their voyage short due to some rough waves and wind. He also knows that once the sun comes back out, the wind will subside and the warmth of the sun will return and make everyone more comfortable.

As the boat skims through the small waves, the sky instead becomes darker with every moment that passes. Dark cumulus clouds usually mean storms. Andrew and Sandy both know that. Corbin too, doesn't like the look of the clouds now so he turns to Andrew and motions for him to come forward. It was not that Corbin hadn't noticed that the skies had been painted in pinks and lavenders this morning. That was the tell tale sign to any captain that a storm was coming. Andrew sees Corbin look to the skies and knows he is concerned. He hurries to the front of the little boat to see what Corbin wants to do.

Corbin tells him that he and Sandy need to move to the front of the boat, into the small cabin. It would be dark down there but warmer, dryer and safer. Fearing the worst now, Andrew shakes his head in agreement and turns to gather Sandy.

Worried now, he makes his way to the bench and reaches for Sandy's hand. She immediately lets him lift her from her seat and follows behind him holding tightly to his hand and her hat. He leads her past Captain Adcock to the little door next to his seat. Corbin doesn't take his eyes off the waters as Andrew opens the door. She follows him below, ducking her head as not to hit it on the low doorframe.

Sandy closes the door behind them as they go into the cabin. The enclosed space is small; in fact, they both have to immediately sit down on the cushions of the V-berth. There isn't enough room for two people to stand together on the floor.

The mattress has a distinct smell of mildew, but the warmth there is welcoming to both of them. Sandy pulls the hat from her head and pushes at her curls to loosen them trying desperately to shake the fear from her mind. Andrew laughs at the site of her hair, more to lighten the mood than to make fun. She smirks at him knowing all too well what her orange bob must look like.

Each of them sitting on opposite sides of the V-berth, they feel the little boat creak as it goes over each wave and slam down as it descends. Soon their bodies get into the rhythm of the boat riding the waves, and they begin to relax. But just as quickly, the wind picks up and starts to whip the small boat around in the water like a toy in a tub; they both become uneasy once again.

Old memories flood into Sandy's mind, washing over her thoughts and carrying her unwillingly to the place she seldom ever goes. Twelve year-old Sandy returns to Henderson Lake where she is desperately searching for Mary.

CHAPTER 12

Memories

The cold water quickly rushes over me as I slide into the icy lake. The stinging cold is quite unexpected. I hold my breath while searching and fighting desperately to reach her as the dark, frigid waters swirl around me. This is a battle I must win.

I see my sister's arm in the murky water below me, and I grab blindly for her in desperation. I hold on to her for a moment and jerk her arm upward. Her face turns towards mine and I see panic in her eyes. Frantically I pull and just as quickly her slippery arm slides out of my hand as my little sister drifts further below me.

I am out of air now. I begin to push and pull myself upward not sure if I will make it to the surface. I do not want to leave my sister down there but the need for air is a necessity I can't control. My chest is hurting, I am not sure if it is the pressure of the deep water or my aching heart.

Finally, my head pops out of the water as I push the insistent oxygen back into my lungs. I take two long breaths before I dive back into the liquid ice again. Frantically searching, I try again and again to find her, coming up to the surface only when I must. Minutes seem like hours. My sister is nowhere in sight.

Finally, exhausted and beaten, I swim under the overturned boat for protection from the driving rains and hail, knowing that Mary is gone. I press my nose into the hull of the boat, and count the remaining seconds of air as water replaces life.

With a sudden jolt of the boat, Sandy's mind returns her to Corbin's boat and to Andrew. Her body shudders with such fierceness that Andrew turns to look into her eyes to see what causes her body to tremble so. Her eyes are swimming with fear. He has no idea that her fear is haunting her from the past.

Sandy watches on the reel of her mind as her own horror show continues to play out before her. Wanting to run from the horrific scene but unable, she continues to replay the scene in her mind over and over. Her greatest fears had been brought up from the depths as she feels herself yielding to them. She sits, frozen in time, not able to move, not able to think, and not able to feel anything but emptiness.

CHAPTER 13

The Funeral

Sandy's Diary

Today is Monday, August 24, 1981. This is the day I have been dreading for the past week. Mary is to be buried today. The house is full of relatives from both sides of the family. Everyone is hiding their smiles and talking in whispers. It all feels so artificial...so hollow. I see the faces of the people that I know, but they are not themselves. They are nothing more than strangers wearing masks of those that I love. I know too that I am concealing my feelings, hiding them from plain view, hoping desperately to disguise the guilt I feel. Even Grandpa is talking in softer than normal shades, hiding his heartache.

The most surprising of all is when Dad, in an uncharacteristically melancholy way, says to me, "I never thought this day would come, Sandy. A father should not be expected to bury his daughter...his youngest...his child." His voice cracks as he tries to get out the next thought, *"I am just not supposed to outlive my child."* His eyes fill with tears and his body is racked by the sobs that follow. I realize that no one is himself during a tragedy, not even my dad. I hug him tightly. I watch as his tears fall down his cheeks and into the corners of his mouth. There is nothing I can say to my dad. He is in a dark place that I assume only a parent can go. I do not feel that my guilt and sadness would ever match up to his, so I do not speak of it. In fact, I don't speak about it to anyone.

I spent most of this morning alone upstairs in my room. I had little interest in greeting all my aunts and uncles, cousins and grandparents that had gathered quietly downstairs. I am worried about Mom. She too, has stayed up in her room, lying in her bed, not wanting to talk to or see anyone, especially me.

I know she blames me for Mary's death. And sometimes she blames Dad. I don't understand that because he wasn't even there. Only I was there. I was the only one that could have saved Mary from drowning and I didn't. Maybe I should have tried harder. Dad suggested that I write down my feelings about Mary and the day she died. That is why I am writing in my diary. I think it is a waste of time, but I will try because I need to be strong for him. And maybe this will make me stronger.

On the day Mary died, we were at the lake. The day started out like any other summer day there. We had arrived at our cabin late the night before and promptly went to bed. As we heard the ducks quacking through our open windows the next morning, we got up to feed them and to see the sunrise over the lake. That was my favorite time of day. I wonder if I will ever have another favorite time of day at the lake again.

I could smell the bacon cooking in the kitchen and ran out to hug Dad. He was in his usual good mood, humming a Beatles' tune, his favorite band, as he fried the eggs and bacon for Mary and me. We ate our breakfast quickly so we could head out to the dock to feed the ducks that swam near our pier waiting for their breakfast. We carried with us the loaf of day-old bread that Mom always packed for them.

Mom couldn't come with us on that weekend. Maybe if she had come, Mary wouldn't be dead. Perhaps Mom blames herself for Mary's death.

She had some charity sale and had to stay home. Sometimes that happened because she was always volunteering for some cause or another. But Mary and I always love coming to the lake and so does Dad. It is our favorite place. Or at least it was.

Mary Virginia, as Mom called her, was eight years old and going into the third grade on the day she died. She is my little sister. I am twelve. Mary and I are a lot alike. We both have flaming red hair, like our dad. And freckles…lot and lots of freckles on our faces, shoulders, and legs. Mary's hair is a tad calmer than mine. People always tell Mary and me that they knew exactly who our daddy is, by the hair. I am always happy when people tell me that.

Mom does not look at all like us. She is the "black beauty" of the family, as Daddy likes to say. She is tall, has "smooth as silk" dark hair and is beautiful. She doesn't even have one freckle or one out-of-control hair on her head. Dad always tells us how lucky he was to find our mom, that she is "just perfect". And we all agree that she is.

Mary and I fight sometimes, but mostly we get along, especially when we are at the lake. Dad got our lake cabin from his twin brother, Uncle Pete. Dad's brother bought the falling down cabin when he finished college. He lived here for two years, making the cabin perfect, that is, until he met Su Lou. That's when Uncle Pete moved away to China to marry her.

I always loved to say Su Lou's name. I wish I had a rhyming name too. When he married Su he gave the cabin to Dad. Our whole family went to China for their wedding. It was beautiful, like Su Lou. Uncle Pete said he didn't see himself ever coming back to Lake Henderson again. He was madly in love and would stay in China forever because Su didn't want to leave her Chinese family. And so far that has been true.

Uncle Pete isn't coming to the funeral either. I am not sure we will ever see Uncle Pete again. We get a Christmas card from him every year and sometimes he and Dad will talk on the phone. Su Lou is really pretty and I can see why he wants to stay in China forever. Uncle Pete was really sorry when Dad called about Mary. Uncle Pete and Su Lou both cried.

Maybe because Uncle Pete gave us this cabin and Dad misses his brother, or maybe because he really does love the outdoors and rugged cabin life, he comes to the lake as much as he can. Mary and I usually come with him. On many days we go out in the rowboat and fish with Dad. He loves to catch and eat them for dinner that same night. "Freshly caught fish are the best," he would say. Mary and I don't like to eat them, but would always go with him 'cause he liked us to come.

Dad always talks of days gone by. Mom used to say he was a young man with an old man's mind and was born in the wrong decade. He loves anything from the 60's or 70's, especially the music that he plays at night on his record player. He wears clothes that are out of date too. He calls them vintage. None of my friends' dads dress like him. One thing I especially love about my dad is that he is very fair about everything and he is always very positive and in a good mood. And sometimes he talks to me like an adult- about stuff like Mary's death and being her dad. Most importantly, he doesn't blame me for Mary's death. He says it was an accident. It could have happened to him or Mom or even Mary. I love my dad.

Mary and I fed the ducks their breakfast that morning and then went back inside the cabin. Dad told us that he had some "projects" to do down in the barn. I think the "barn", as he calls it, is really a boathouse. I guess since we don't have a big boat, just a small rowboat, he decided to change its name and function, turning it into the barn. He stores all kinds of things, mostly stuff that Mom doesn't want in the garage at home. She always called it Dad's junk pile. He loves his old junk.

School will be starting soon for Mary and me. Our time coming to the cabin with Dad will be ending soon. I had wanted to explore the little island that is around the spit of land that is next to our slew. Mary and I talked about going there all summer and now that summer was about over, I told Mary that today was the day. We are going to take the boat out and go exploring.

Mary was excited and ran to the bedroom to get her extra large straw hat out of the closet. Mom had trained us well, She always said, "You girls have fair skin, like your dad's, so you must always wear a hat to protect it. Ladies don't want leather skin!" I never really understood what she meant about leather skin. But since I loved to wear hats, I did what she told me. Most of the time, I wear one of Dad's caps. He always gives me his old ones that Mom has shrunk in the dryer.

I followed Mary into the bedroom and dug around and could only find my cowboy hat. I dragged it out from under my bed. I ran into the kitchen and got two apples, a jar of peanut butter and a butter knife, and filled two bottles with water. Prepared as we could be for exploring, off to the boat we went.

It was a pretty day when we started out, with small clouds hanging in the sky. Mary and I knew how to paddle. Dad had taught us two years ago and we would go out with him at least once a day and help him paddle when we are at the lake. I thought we were ready for our solo trip.

After we got into the boat and pushed it off the shore, we rowed it over to the barn. We steered it into the barn through a large opening on the lakeside. Dad was surprised to see us there. He told us that he was proud that we maneuvered the boat over from the shore. I told him about our plans and he stopped hammering for a minute and thought about it.

Finally, he said, "Sandy, you are twelve, right?"

"Of course I am. You know that, silly!"

"Well then, I think you are responsible enough to paddle over to Goat Island and back with your sister. Go, have fun girls. Don't be gone too long and watch out for those goats."

He laughed loudly and turned back to his hammering. I know now he wished he had never said those words to us.

He waved as we headed off on our adventure. We paddled out into the middle of our slew. We had to go out pretty far into the lake to get around the spit of land to that side. When we were rounding the point of land, I remembered something important. We didn't put the life jackets in the boat.

Sometimes Dad didn't make us wear them, but they were always in the boat. Mom always made sure that we had them on, her #1 rule. I stopped paddling and thought for a second about going back to get them, but decided against it knowing we had never needed them before. That was the worst decision of my life.

As we rounded the spit of land we could see the little island. Dad always called it Goat Island although it didn't really have a name. People said there were goats living on that island and I really wanted to see for myself.

Mary and I started looking for the goats the minute the island came into view. We couldn't see any. As the island got closer and closer to us, we still couldn't see the goats, so we decided to run the boat ashore so we could go exploring on the far side of the island, thinking that perhaps the goats were grazing over there.

Mary and I climbed out of the boat when we hit the pebbles and pulled it further onto the rocky shore. Together we started exploring. In a matter of minutes we had walked over to the far side of the small island. There were a few trees there and some mud next to the water's edge and rocks…lots and lots of all sizes of rocks. Besides that, there was nothing else. Disappointed, we soon realized that there was no treasure, no islanders, and most importantly, no goats. Dad would have to rename the island.

After our disappointing exploration, we decided to get back into the boat and eat our snack. We began to get bored and I noticed that bigger clouds had formed in the sky further out on the lake. Some of them blocked the sun. It felt slightly cooler and somehow the weather and the fact that we didn't find any goats dampened my mood. I suggested we head back to the cabin. Mary agreed as I pushed the boat out into the lake.

Mary was chatting away about her best friend, Molly, as we paddled. The wind began to blow and little white caps formed on the water's surface. When we were out in the middle of the lake ready to turn towards our slew, I decided that we needed to paddle harder cause the wind was starting to push the rowboat backwards. Mary tried and complained that her arms were hurting. I could see that we were making little progress. And the small boat was being pushed further into the deeper part of the lake by a stiff breeze.

I began to get worried when the wind started howling. Within minutes, the clouds turned dark. I knew a storm was brewing and we needed to be on shore NOW. Then the rain came. Mary was complaining about her arms and now too, the fact that she was getting wet. And she stopped paddling. As the rain got even stronger, it became more difficult to see where we were going through the sheet of water. I could barely make out the shore in the distance as we suddenly were in a grey fog.

As the lake turned gray and violent, I desperately tried to row. I don't really know what happened next except that I lost one of the paddles. I think my hands were wet because of the rain and it slid out of my hand and into the water. The choppy water and wind swept the paddle behind us and it was gone. Now, we were left with just one big paddle, and Mary's tiny one. I knew we were in trouble.

My heart began to race and Mary started to cry and slid over to sit next to me on my bench. I put my arm around her shoulders. When Mary came over next to me, the boat rocked hard to the left, which allowed lake water to pour inside. Now with water surrounding our feet up to our knees, the boat sat much lower in the water.

Dad had shown me the stopper once when I had asked him what it was for. He told me that you pull it to let water out of the bottom of the boat. I remembered his words and I quickly pulled it out. That was a terrible mistake. I knew it the moment I pulled it out. Water filled the boat and I knew it was sinking.

As the waves in the lake pushed us around, Mary was propelled out into the lake. It all happened in an instant of time. And in that one instant of time, she was gone. Desperately I tried to grab her. I swam below looking for my little sister. The water was cloudy. And when I poked my head up out of the lake, I found the fog thick as smoke. Mud and debris from the bottom of the lake seemed to be mixed with the water and made it murky and impossible to see. I swam up to the foggy surface and back down to look for her over and over and over again. Finally, exhausted, I found the boat floating upside down and swam underneath for protection from the hail that was now falling. When I knew my air was running out, I took one last breath.

I woke up in my room. Dad was sitting on the bed next to me. Surprised, I sat straight up. "Where is Mary, is she okay?" I screamed.

"Shhh, it's okay, Sandy, it's going to be okay."

I looked around our room but couldn't find her. "Dad! Is she okay?" I asked again.

Dad held my hand and told me that she was missing. That they had found me on Goat Island with my face in the mud holding onto Mary's straw hat, but Mary was nowhere to be found.

…And that was it. That was almost a week ago. They say her body washed up on the shore several miles from our cabin several days after the day she died. Dad says we aren't having an open casket. I am glad. I don't want to see the fear in Mary's eyes and the disappointment there.

When the time came to leave the house for the funeral, I finally drug myself down the stairs to the kitchen. Everyone wanted to hug me and smiled even though I know their smiles meant nothing. I didn't want to smile back so I didn't. Daddy came up to me and put his arm around my shoulders so I would feel safe. I needed to feel safe.

Mom was the last to come down and get into the car. She looked dreadful. Her eyes were red and puffy. It looked as if she hadn't brushed her hair all week. It was frizzy and matted. She had on an old black dress that was wrinkled. When I saw her, I knew things were bad. We drove to the funeral home in silence. Mom would sniff every few minutes and wipe her nose with Grandpa's hanky. Dad just stared straight ahead at the road. Uncle Spence, Dad's other brother, drove the car.

Lots of people were at the funeral. Most of the town came. As Dad said, everyone is very sad when it is a child that dies. They all came because it was so sad. I know they all blame me.

At the graveside, when the dirt was thrown over Mary's casket, I finally cried. That was the first time I cried for Mary. I cried because it was so permanent, so forever. And at that moment, I knew it was real. I wouldn't see my little sister again. I wouldn't hear her voice and I would be alone. I was supposed to throw my rose in the grave then but I didn't. I held on to it. Mom turned and squinted her eyes at me, like I was stabbing her in the heart, but Dad put his arm around my shoulders. I knew it would be okay.

We turned and left that day before the casket was all the way in the ground. I guess they do that cause it is too sad. I think of Mary in that dark casket now and again and worry about her. I hope she doesn't know she is in there 'cause she would be scared. And, most of all, I hope she knows that I love her and I tried to find her.

CHAPTER 14

Return to Safety

Sitting in the hull of Corbin's boat, Sandy recalls those nightmarish memories of long ago as if they happened yesterday. The memories are as vivid to her now just as if she was still that young girl at Henderson Lake. It was saddest time in her life and she tries to push them aside whenever she can. But being here, on the ocean, in a storm, brought it all back. She had dusted off the cobwebs to relive them again. Memories of that time are exhausting. All Sandy wants now is to be hugged like she had been all those years ago by her daddy.

Almost on cue, Andrew gets up from his side of the berth and sits close to her. He puts his arm tightly around her shoulders, holding her as she cries. His words of consolation do little good, as she can't stop the tears from falling.

The boat continues to be pounded by the waves. Sandy hopes the rainstorm will drown out the sounds of her sobs. But, Andrew hears. He knows she is afraid. Her fear is real; he can see it in the blue of her eyes. Her fear though is not entirely what Andrew thinks it is.

Up above them on the deck of the boat, Corbin continues his battle with the sea.

Andrew asks Sandy to tell him why she is so upset. He thinks it is his fault for taking her on a boat ride and he begins to apologize. Sandy shakes her head and puts her finger to his lips stopping his apology. More than anything, she wants to reassure him that it is not *this* boat ride that has her upset.

Never having shared her feelings about that dreadful day with anyone but her father and Jim, Sandy tells Andrew about Mary and the day she died. Tears fall as she talks. When her story is done, she holds up the wet straw hat that she had held securely onto all day. "This straw hat is very precious to me. It belonged to Mary. I was gripping it tightly when they found me unconscious on the shore of Goat Island. On that fateful day, I couldn't grab hold of my sister, but isn't it ironic that I made sure I held onto her hat."

With a deep breath Sandy continues, "My sweet daddy says that he thinks that that was a sign from Mary saying, 'my death was not your fault, Sandy. It was an accident. I love you and want you to wear my hat whenever you need comfort.' I believe what my daddy said all those years ago, is true. So I wear her hat whenever I need to feel her with me. Today was one of those days."

Finally victorious, Capt. Corbin is able to guide his boat and its passengers to safely. As the boat is safely in the harbor, the wind and sea calm, and rain starts to subside, and Sandy starts to relax in Andrew's arms. He holds her for a long time.

Corbin turns off the engine as Andrew says to Sandy, "I am here, Sandy, I am here for you." Feeling safe once again, both physically and mentally, her thoughts of that day so long ago start to subside and she takes comfort from Andrew.

Corbin gives a shout to Andrew from above saying, "All clear folks, come on up and see the sun!" Andrew smiles at Sandy and pulls her gently up off the berth. "Let's go and make some *good* memories, Sandy." Andrew whispers to her as they come up out of the cabin.

CHAPTER 15

Love Speech

The rain clouds blow to the north and the sun decides to stay out, allowing Andrew and Sandy to continue with their day of exploration and shopping. They dine for lunch at Dave's Lobster Pot and continue to shop the afternoon away holding hands and enjoying each other's company.

Late that afternoon, Corbin's boat rounds the last bend in the shoreline, taking them back to where they began this long day of boating. All three of the sailors are tired and very glad to be back on dry land. Andrew and Sandy thank Corbin for the boat tour and climb into Andrew's truck to head back to the cottage.

With their emotions on overdrive, and their bodies cold from the wind and rain, a hot shower seemed like the perfect end to this very eventful day. Happy to have them back home, Toby excitedly greets them at the truck. With the clouds gone, the late afternoon sky begins to turn lighter shades of orange and pink as they once again marvel at the beauty it holds.

After her shower, Sandy puts on a cozy sweatshirt and jeans and meets Andrew in the kitchen. The couple work together on dinner, preparing a salad and sautéing some large scallops and shrimp that they had picked up at the seafood market on the way home. They relax by the fire, sitting close as they eat their meal, continuing to enjoy each other's company.

After dinner, the two grab another glass of wine and begin chatting about life and love. Sandy asks Andrew about his childhood and his many 'loves' he has had over the years. Laughing, he stands up before her with his wine in hand, and begins his soliloquy, "Well, my sweet, let me tell you about LOVE. That one single word seemed to occupy my mind for so much of my life. But now, I have come to realize at the tender age of forty-five, that love really has been so absent for so much of my life. Where shall I begin this delightful tale of love and lust? Perhaps I need something stronger to drink."

Sandy laughs and looks to the bookshelf where she sees a decanter and two small glasses. She walks over and says, "Will this do?"

"Why yes, I think a little cognac is just the thing I need to get through this saga." They clink together their glasses and Andrew begins.

"Let us begin with the most lovely Miss James."

She laughs, and questions, "Miss James?"

"Yes." Andrew goes on to say, "The *lovely* Miss James."

Continuing with his oration, he tells about his journey with love or the absence thereof. "It all began when I was a young eighth grade middle school boy. I was worldly, debonair, and shorter than most of the girls in my grade."

Sandy snickers making small bubbles in her glass.

Clearing his throat, Andrew continues, "I remember the day well. My new English teacher, Miss James, spoke to me on the first day of class in her sexy, raspy voice. She looked into my eyes with her blue orbs, and that was *it*! She desired me and I could feel the lust in her gaze. In a blinding flash, I was *in love*."

Andrew sighs and dramatically gazes into space. "During that entire year in school and out of school, I dreamed of her, and thought of her, every waking moment. I just knew my love for her was true. I noticed every single thing about her, from the different hues of her new hair colors that she changed each month, down to the new pointed red leather heels that she wore on her delicate feet. And most importantly, I noticed her beautiful curves."

Sandy giggles at his description of the teacher's shoes and curves, but tells him to go on totally enjoying his "love speech".

Andrew continues, "I studied her and knew her and obsessed over her. She was perfect. Whenever she spoke to me or came near, my heart beat faster, big drops of sweat would pour from my forehead, and I stammered, unable to speak. There were even times that I was rendered unable to leave the shelter of my desk."

"OK…" Sandy laughs out loud this time, "*That* I believe!"

"Don't laugh…this is serious," Andrew fires back with just a hint of mischief in his eyes. "This was love, so I thought. I couldn't tell you anything about verb tense or conjugation I learned in her class that year, but I sure could tell you everything there was to know about Miss James. For me, summer arrived all too soon that year. With its arrival, Miss James departed from my life, leaving me heart broken with a gigantic hole in my young and vulnerable heart. I never saw her again. I heard years later that other boys were also in love with her, and it was rumored that she may have fallen for one of them too."

Sandy giggles, "Oh no! Go on, Andrew."

"Ginny came along in 9th grade. She was my biology lab partner. She was a cute girl with a great body and curly hair… not unlike your own," Andrew winks starting to feel the cognac as his story begins to take on its own life.

"She bounced everywhere she went and that part of her really attracted me…you know the bouncing around part." He laughs. "Ginny and I flirted with each other in lab for the first month of school and I eventually asked her to homecoming. She went with me and we became a couple in the back seat of Stan's Honda that night. It was love, or so I thought. For two years, Ginny and I were together. Thinking back on it, I stayed with Ginny longer than I stayed with anyone else that I was in love with, until Beth."

He pauses and darts his eyes quickly to Sandy, wishing he hadn't mentioned Beth. Sandy smiles. "Go on, Andrew," she says.

Getting more serious now, Andrew continues although not quite sure if he is enjoying this conversation so much anymore. "I was very happy and content with Ginny, until Susan entered my life in eleventh grade. I met her at a concert. I had gone with some buddies to this local club and met her there. She captivated my heart from the moment I saw her. She was quite the opposite of Ginny. She was what I would call a rocker chick.

She had jet-black hair, deep dark eyes, dark clothing, black tattoos and a dark heart. And I fell madly in love with her. Her starkness and independence fascinated me, and I had to be with her. She was several years older than me, and not the type of girl I would take home to meet Mom. But she really did totally fascinate me.

We saw each other whenever we could. It was somewhat difficult because she lived in an apartment with some other girls on the Southside, and I still had to go to high school. It was an odd relationship. I idolized her though. And I also learned from her that love can be dark and demeaning."

With his mood becoming somewhat darker, Andrew goes on.

"I was so taken with her that my love became an obsession. I think it is strange how obsession and love can get confused sometimes. But Susan, on the other hand, told me, after only two months of dating, that she loved me and that I fulfilled *some* of her needs, but not *all* of her needs. She wanted an open relationship; both of us free to date other people. I had no interest in dating anyone else. Her love was conditional and present only when it was convenient for her. I soon realized that my love was not shared at all by her, and that actually it wasn't love at all. When I realized all of these things, I sadly and with a defeated heart, left her. I did not date for an entire year after Susan."

Realizing that he was getting introspective and somewhat depressed, Sandy stands to pour another glass of cognac and says, "So, Susan does not sound like your type anyway. Let's forget about her. Let me get this straight. There was Miss James-your first love, Ginny, Susan, and then.... COLLEGE!" Andrew's eyes light up when she says that word and his mood lightens.

After pouring each of them another glass, Sandy sits down to listen more intently.

He begins with a smile, "Yes, then there is college...with its many, many, varied and gorgeous women. You know my college years became a blur of women to me. There were so many women; each one beautiful, each one sexy, and each one wanting me...at least my ego told me that. Obviously, there is no accounting for good or bad taste," he laughs and continues, "The rumors you heard about me are true, you know, all of them!" He goes on to say, "During those four wondrous years, I jumped from one woman to the next, from one bed to the next, and so on and so on. Women seemed to flock towards me; I guess I was just that good looking," Andrew tries to say with a straight face, but failing. "So, anyway, I took full advantage."

Sandy interrupts him for a minute, "Yes you did, and yes you are right, you were a good-looking guy then." At that point she starts giggling and the giggles grow into a full laugh.

"Then? What about *now*??" Andrew laughs and reaches over and tickles her behind her knee. "My dashing looks have always been an acquired taste anyways," he says with a mocked pain in his voice.

"How did you know that is my tickle spot?" she screams in laughter. "And yes, I will admit, I even thought you were extremely good looking, and I was dating Jim at the time. Shame on me! Now, go on with your story."

They both laugh.

"You always had your choice of the best-looking women on campus, and you lived a fast and furious life then, didn't you?" she asked Andrew in a serious tone.

"Yeah, maybe...I don't know. I was young and I was cocky. At that age, young and cocky are more than enough to get you in trouble. But you, young lady, you were a calming, constant influence in my life during college. Did you know that? And you were off limits to me, way out of reach for me, because of Jim. I loved Jim. I saw the relationship between the two of you and I envied it. I didn't really understand it, and didn't really want it at the time. But I could see true love in both of your eyes."

Determined not to tear up again, Sandy said, "Awe...that is really sweet, Andrew. I didn't know you felt that way about me back then. And yes, Jim and I were very much in love in college."

"So, to continue," Andrew says, "at this point in my life, I didn't believe in love, at least for me. I somehow knew I had no idea of what love really was. Love was not a word in my vocabulary or a feeling in my heart. I did what felt good at the moment. That is how I lived my life during those years. That was it. My love life was a series of one-night stands and no commitments. I was Andrew, the good-looking man of impulse and thrill. That was me...*then*.

It is so sad, really as I look back on those years. I was lost. Lost in myself. Lost without direction, not able to decipher what love was or how to get it. As a result, the women I dated became boring, and more and more of a chore to me; I became hardened and callused towards them, and eventually callused towards life in general.

But, I must tell you Sandy, and I hope this doesn't make you upset, but that fateful Thanksgiving holiday in Dallas became a big turning point in my life. You and Jim had invited me down for Thanksgiving; my two favorite people in the entire world asked me to join them for one of my favorite holidays. That is when I kissed my best friend's wife.

Afterwards, I felt so low and despicable. You weren't just another woman to kiss and throw away. You were Sandy, my best friend's wife and my good friend too. I knew it was wrong in my heart, but that one kiss on that Thanksgiving sent a little spark deep down inside of me. It penetrated my empty heart. That little spark found its way to my hardened heart changing everything for me. I can't explain it. That catalyst put life back into my heart. Sandy, I have wanted to tell you that for so very long."

Sandy sat very still sipping her cognac and patting his hand. Andrew struggled to read her face. He hoped that he was not saying too much.

"I stayed so confused after that holiday. I couldn't decide whether this spark was love or desire. I didn't know which. After that kiss, I went home with the tiny little bit of life glowing deep down in this heart and it began to grow. That is when I realized I had to see you again. This new feeling in my heart was addicting. The feeling of life and love and hope and warmth was back. I suddenly realized at that time that my heart had been so cold, so empty, and so lifeless for so many, many years. I was truly alive for the first time in what seemed to be a lifetime.

Your invitation to come back at Christmas seemed too good to be true. I always wondered if it had been your idea or Jim's to invite me back."

Toby suddenly jumps up on the couch and interrupts Andrew's thought.

"You need to go out, Bud?" he asks Toby. Toby wags his tail and barks until he gets up. Sandy stands and together they walk towards the door to take Toby out. Andrew reaches over to hold Sandy's hand, and the two walk down the road wondering what is in store for them tomorrow.

CHAPTER 16

Living on the Streets

Beth and her new friend continue riding the train headed to Nashville. Beth continues telling her life story.

"For the next few years, I lived in smelly boxes, doorways, and under fire escapes on streets in various cities with the drunks, addicts and whores. That was my middle school and high school education; an education that forced me to grow up too fast and too hard.

At some point during my first few years on the streets, I realized that Melody had been right. I wished I could talk to my best friend and tell her. The streets were not a safe place for a young teenager. Evil and broken people lived on the streets, and I would have been better off with the nuns in the orphanage.

My first sexual encounter happened in a refrigerator box on 23rd Street in Boston. Finding that large sturdy box was one of my happiest moments while living on 23rd. I dragged the flattened box with every ounce of energy I had, to 'my spot' under the train trusses and set it up. I was really proud of my 'home'. It was warm, dry, and the best part, a place where I could sit or sleep and be alone. It was big and had enough space for all my worldly belongings.

He, my first encounter, decided one stormy night that he wanted my home and me, and in that order. So, he crawled right inside to make himself comfortable. I was a slight fourteen-year-old feisty thing, and completely confidant that I could force him out. I was wrong.

With a few kicks and punches to my face in the first horrific moments, he forced himself into the box and then on top of me. His smelly alcohol breath and sweaty, soaking-wet body was all over me. I fought hard, but he was too big and strong. He raped me over and over. At some point I went unconscious. I remember his bearded face with his toothless mouth and his whiskey breath. That gut-wrenching experience still is a vivid memory today.

I don't know why he chose to leave that night. He must have thought that he heard someone or else he did not think that I was worth the trouble to drag out onto the street. So, he left me for dead that night in the refrigerator box. And dead I would be if it hadn't been for Dorothy Chapman."

Beth looks over at her companion. She is shaking her head and sighing. "You poor dear," she whispers almost in tears.

Feeling the woman's sorrow, she continues, "Dorothy Chapman was strolling down 23rd Street, her normal route to work, when she spotted the river of crimson and its tributaries flowing downstream out of the box. She looked inside, thinking there might be an injured animal there, only to see me unconscious in a pool of my own blood. Dorothy Chapman immediately called 911, and I was taken to Grace Memorial Hospital.

When I woke up, Melody was sitting by my hospital bed and she was holding my hand. I looked for a long time into her face. She was older but I knew it was she. I couldn't understand where she had come from, and how she knew I was there. She talked to me for a while and then told me that she wanted me to have a better life. She said that the only way I could do that was to trust people. I had to open up my heart and let others in. She said that things would get better for me if I tried to do that. All she wanted was for me to find happiness. I held her hand for a long time as I drifted into and out of sleep.

Grace Memorial Hospital was where my life took a turn for the better. Dorothy was a very generous and kind woman. From the moment she saw me lying unconscious in the box on 23rd, she took it upon herself to help me in any way she could.

Upon my release from the hospital, Dorothy bought me new clothes, took me out to lunch in a restaurant and asked me what I wanted to do with my life. I was a fourteen year old girl that didn't have a family, didn't have an education, and hadn't a clue as to what I wanted in life.

But I followed Melody's advice, and tried to trust this stranger that had just entered my life.

Once again, a new situation found me, but this time it was a good situation. Dorothy took me to her apartment on 64th Street. There, she made her guest room into my room. I had never had my own room before."

Taking a deep breath, Beth goes on.

"It was really hard at first; I didn't want to trust Dorothy Chapman. So far, there had been no adult that had ever taken any interest in me whatsoever, and I was not sure that this stranger would either. But I listened to my friend, Melody, my voice of reason.

I must admit I was terrible to Dorothy. For the first several weeks I acted out just to see how she would react. Time after time, Dorothy returned my meanness and horrible behavior with kindness. It took weeks for me to finally trust her.

One night, I came into the living room where she was finishing up some work, and asked her if I could go to school. She smiled up at me and told me that she had been waiting for me to ask her. She enrolled me in school the next morning like she said she would. I enrolled in eighth Grade. It seemed to me that everything she said she would do for me, she did. From that day on, I stopped being difficult and began to trust her."

Beth looks into the eyes of the old woman saying the words aloud to her that she had never voiced before, "I love Dorothy Chapman. She was my savior but more importantly, my mother." After saying those words, Beth pauses for a moment as her emotions surge.

"Love is a wonderful thing, isn't it Beth?" the woman says as she smiles.

Beth shakes her head and continues with her story. "The school was only a few blocks from our apartment building. I could walk each morning and each afternoon. Dorothy was a dentist and was very busy. She had no children of her own and treated me as if I was her own flesh and blood, which was something I never quite understood. It was a relationship made in heaven for me. She introduced me to church and I went every time the doors were open.

I had a fantastic life with Dorothy. I loved learning and soon advanced to the ninth grade with honors and then after that, to the tenth grade, signing up for all honors classes. Dorothy couldn't have been prouder of me. Because of her, I became proud of myself, *and* my smile. I finally had a family and a mom that loved me."

Beth stops once again, remembering Dorothy. She continues.

"It was a frigid winter's night, a night where no one walked the streets. Even the homeless sought shelter. And on that night my contented existence with Dorothy Chapman crumbled around me." Tears filled her eyes. "Dorothy didn't come home from work."

With her heart racing Beth spat out her next words in great succession, trying desperately to get through the next part of her story. "I waited for her until midnight when I called the police. After hours of not hearing a thing from anyone, a woman officer knocked on the apartment door the next morning. I let her in. I could tell by her demeanor that she had bad news for me. I could not bear to hear what she had to say.

She sat me down and told me that Dorothy had been mugged, raped, and stabbed by a homeless man on 23rd Street, and had been rushed to Grace Memorial hospital. She had died on the operating table hours before. No one from the hospital knew that I existed, so they did not call. She told me that they caught the homeless man that killed Dorothy right away. He was in jail and that he would probably stay there for the remainder of his years.

I learned later at the attorney's office, that in fact, Dorothy Chapman hadn't told anyone about me, including her estranged family. When the Will was read, I sat there in the lawyer's office with her family, listening to every detail. There was not one mention of me at all.

If Dorothy Chapman could reflect on the night of her death and afterwards, I think she would say she only made one mistake in regards to me.

Her one mistake was *not* the fact that she travelled down and got raped and killed on 23rd Street on her way home from work that night. She would say, that her murder was meant to be because it put that evil homeless drunkard murderer, the one that lived in a stolen blood stained refrigerator box under the train trusses' in jail, on death row, for the rest of his life.

Dorothy would say that her one and only mistake in regards to me was that she didn't write me, her daughter, into her will. And I believe that to this day.

After that afternoon in the attorney's office I realized quite suddenly that social services would be coming for me soon. And because I had no money of my own, I hurried back to Dorothy's apartment and loaded up what I could of my personal belongings and the little bit of cash that I knew Dorothy had hidden in the container by her bed.

I headed out to the streets of Boston once again. Every day I watched our apartment from across the street and soon witnessed Dorothy's family clear out all her belongings. Afterwards a *For Sale* sign went up in the window of our apartment.

I was sixteen years old and heartbroken. Not heartbroken over the money, but broken-hearted over the loss of the only person in the world that ever loved me."

Pausing her story, Beth looks over to the old woman sitting next to her on the train. She is fast asleep. Beth pulls the lady's pink coat up over her shoulder, and then looks out the window watching the landscape as it races past.

Her life is like that landscape, she thinks, fleeting quickly…but hopefully now in a positive direction, and to *him*.

She allows her thoughts to turn to a stranger, the gorgeous man she fell in love with as a sixteen year-old girl. Her circumstances at the time lead her to him; the attractive musician, the man with no name. Fate had brought him to her then and now she goes to him.

Beth feels excitement, an emotion she rarely has felt over her life, welling up inside her, as she sits, riding this Nashville bound train into her future. "Andrew Morgan." Beth says, saying his name aloud. It is a name she had only learned a few months ago. That man, Andrew Morgan, would change her life.

She thinks back on the circumstances that lead up to their first meeting. In a matter of a few weeks, she had gone from Dorothy's nice upscale apartment to the nasty streets of Boston, once again, foraging for food, shelter, and warmth. She remembered the deep sadness and loneliness, as well as the fear that had come back as she returned to the streets. She can remember sitting on the curb where the rainwater overwhelmed the gutters, as she waited to die.

But, she did not die. Instead, she remained half frozen, half starved, with a bruised heart that was barely zoetic. The winter that year in Boston was horrifically cold and wet. She had questioned fate, and wondered why she had been allowed to love someone that would be taken so suddenly from her.

She spent her days wandering the streets or sitting on the curb, and her nights fearing for her life. The day finally came where she found some refuge. Darkness was upon the day once again, and she knew what that meant. She had to find shelter and safety from the weather, and from the people that lurked after dark. The city streets were no place for a teenage girl once the sun goes down. She had learned that a long time ago, and had become quite adept at learning lessons.

One evening, walking as quickly as she could without appearing afraid, an emotion she tried hard to hide most of the time, she headed down a dark alley. It had started raining and she needed to find shelter quickly.

She approached a heavy metal door, adorned with so much graffiti that the grey paint beneath it was barely visible. There was a broom handle stuck in the hinge of the door to keep it open. Looking around the alley and seeing no one, she finally allowed a sigh of relief to escape from her lips. This retreat, in St. Mary's Cathedral would do nicely for the night. Happy to have found such protection, she opened the door further and quickly went inside. It was warm, dark and quiet in the room. Perhaps her soul might find the much needed refuge here too.

She allowed the door to close behind her, accidentally letting it bang against the broom handle. Slowly, she allowed her eyes time to adjust to the semi-dark room. Quickly she realized that she was in the boiler room of the church. Behind the gray metal door was her sanctuary, a small warm room, dimly lit by a fire. The small fire filled the base of a giant boiler. Not only did the aged boiler provide heat for her, but light as well.

Beth can still hear the tune the man whistled that night as he came in the door from the alley moments later. Fearing the worst, she remembered scurrying to the shadows to hide. A large black man in a worn out pair of jeans and flannel shirt pulled open the door, and then pulled the handle of the broom from the door hinges, allowing it to slam shut.

He continued to whistle as he held his cigar and put a large garbage can next to the stairs. Beth remained very quiet as she watched the man. He had an unlit cigar dangling from the corner of his mouth one minute, and then he whistled the next. He whistled one tune after another as he went about the business of tidying up the semi-dark room.

After about ten minutes of straightening the room, He meticulously balanced his cigar on edge of a box beside his chair, pulled out a lunch box and sat in the old creaking rocking chair that was lined with worn out cushions. His chair faced the pile of blankets she was hiding behind so Beth sat down, afraid he might see her.

His whistling continued up until the time he pulled a sandwich from his box and pulled the baggie apart. Even though she couldn't see it, bologna has a very distinct smell and she knew what it was the minute he opened the bag. She had eaten many bologna sandwiches in her past. Her stomach rumbled then, thinking of the smell of the sandwich, just as it did when she was a girl at the orphanage.

After devouring his sandwich, Beth could hear the rustling of the baggie as he put it back into the lunchbox. In a minute or two, she could hear the sound of him munching on a bag of potato chips. She remembers her mouth watering, as she too could smell and taste the salty chip in her mind.

Finally with curiosity getting the best of her, Beth remembered looking out from behind her hiding place to see the man getting an apple from his lunchbox. He didn't eat it; instead he stuffed it into his pocket. He looked at the clock mounted on the wall and began his whistling again. Standing up, he switched off the light bulb over his head and then grabbed the giant garbage can by its handle. Slowly with his lunch box and garbage can he climbed up the creaky old steps. A light from a bulb that illuminated the staircase lit his way. At the top of stairs, he flipped off the switch for the light and closed the heavy door loudly behind him.

The only light remaining in the room now came from the small fire in the furnace. Beth remembers creeping cautiously out from behind the pile of clothes and blankets as she listened to his fading footsteps above her. Once the footsteps completely disappeared, she reached for the string dangling from the light bulb in the rafters. Light filled the space once again.

Knowing that her presence was a secret from Mr. Night Janitor she finally relaxed as she pulled her dinner out of her backpack. Mr. Burt had given her food, just like he did every evening.

Remembering the kindness of the chef and owner of Burt's Restaurant, she smiles. He kept her from starving on those cold Boston nights. She didn't realize how generous that was of him back then. Not only did he give her large portions of whatever food he had left, he always included a plastic fork and napkin as well. Somehow, that little gesture made her feel important.

Feeling thankful for his kindness, and the food, she recalls the prayer she recited every evening before eating Mr. Bert's food; a little prayer she learned from the nuns at St. Cecelia's. "Thank you God in heaven for this food, for this shelter, and for your grace. Amen."

Becoming nostalgic she thinks of Mr. Night Janitor again with fondness. That warm and safe boiler room was her home for many months. She made sure when she ventured out during the day that she left the broom handle in the hinges of the metal door, and then before he arrived at work each night she would pull it out and hide in her secret place. She watched him silently every night as he cleaned, emptied the trash and ate his dinner under the single light bulb. He became her constant friend even though he didn't know it or at least she thought he never knew she was there. His routine kept her company on those cold and lonely nights. The night janitor and Beth got along quite well.

She began to hum those unforgotten tunes keeping time with the click, click, clicking of the train riding along the tracks.

CHAPTER 17

The Nightmare

Sandy wakes with a start to the sound of Andrew's truck engine humming quietly. She listens closer as the truck jumps into gear, whining as it backs away from the cottage. Now in silence, Sandy begins to remember her dream.

The dream starts out to be a lovely one where she and Andrew are running through a meadow, holding hands and laughing. There is music playing in the distance making it a magical scene. She looks to the snow covered peaks waiting for Julie Andrews and the children to come skipping across the mountain slope at any minute harmonizing as they sing, "The hills are alive with the sound of music". The two lovers are laughing and running in the meadow together, blissfully happy. She has a feeling of euphoria and begs for her fantasy dream to continue.

Euphoria quickly changes to fear, as circumstances in her dream suddenly change for the worse. The bright sunlit sky begins to darken and a pernicious dark-haired woman with snake-like eyes is suddenly and almost magically in their way. She hovers ever so slightly above the ground as she holds her arms out to the sides of her body. Her dark clothing drapes like a witch's black cape from her arms. This woman calls out to Andrew as if she is casting a spell over him. She continues to block their way as the sky becomes stormy.

All around Sandy the grasses in the meadow move frantically back and forth bowing to the wind as it begins to howl. There is nowhere for her and Andrew to hide to get out of the unnatural tempest and away from this woman who grows larger with each passing moment. Becoming omnipresent, the woman looms over them; a menacing black figure seeking justice and revenge, but for what, Sandy doesn't know.

Andrew does not seem afraid of her, in fact he is watching her with a look of adoration, not fear. The evil-looking woman's eyes turn a stone cold green as if they are hardened emeralds. She reaches for Andrew's right hand. Sandy quickly grabs his left hand to keep him from following, thus beginning a tug of war over him. Andrew has become the prize.

His arms begin to stretch as each of them pulls him to their side. His arms stretch to grotesque lengths. Sandy finally realizes that if she continues to pull in the manner she is, Andrew would stretch out across the meadow and perhaps break in two. She lets go of him.

The witchy woman with emerald eyes continues to hold tightly onto Andrew. His arms, like giant rubber bands spring back to shape. Sandy loses sight of him as he snaps back to the other side of the meadow. In that moment the sky clears, the sun shines again and Sandy knows that Andrew is gone. The dark-haired woman has won.

In her dream, Sandy sits down in the meadow and begins to cry because she has lost Andrew forever. Hearing the sound of an engine in the distance, she jumps up and runs towards the noise hoping to find him.

Sandy wakes suddenly as her tears and the meadow disappear. She realizes that the sound in her dream is really Andrew's truck engine as he backs away from the cottage. Her sad and grief-stricken heart relaxes. She is glad she is awake and it was just a nightmare. She looks to the bedroom window.

Once again, the day greets her with blue skies. Cobalt blue fills in the panes and overtakes her room bringing a brightness and beauty that grabs at her heart and lightens her mood. "How can I lay here worrying over a silly nightmare when this beautiful day awaits." she says aloud as she shakes the nightmarish woman from her head.

It was her third day on the island with Andrew. She didn't want to waste one minute of time. Upon entering the kitchen, Sandy is greeted with aroma of brewed coffee, her favorite morning smell. She looks around the open cottage knowing he will be nowhere to be found. After filling her coffee cup, she opens the front door to confirm what she already knows. Andrew and Toby have gone to run an errand. "They must have driven to the store for something," she says to herself. Carrying her overly full coffee cup back to her room, she sets it carefully on the dresser. Throwing on a pair of jeans, sweatshirt and jacket she makes her way back to the front door of the cottage as she sips her coffee. Without much thought, she makes the decision to take an early morning walk around Andrew's property.

With refilled coffee mug in hand, Sandy closes the front door behind her and surveys the area. There, constant in its presence and beauty is the ocean surrounding the cottage. She is amazed that after three days of being in its company, the view still takes her breath away. Her love/hate relationship with the sea continues. She stares out into it focusing on the dim line separating the sky and the water.

Although difficult to do, Sandy finally turns her back to the ocean ignoring its magical allure. She looks ahead towards the dirt driveway as she studies the magnificent pine tree forest guarding either side. She spots an almost forgotten pathway through the trees to the left of the drive and decides to follow it instead of taking the more obvious way.

Pine needles lay on the path making it a cushion for easier walking. The fresh pine branches close her in, leaving their scent heavy in the air. Sandy breathes deeply to take in its earthy fragrance. Her sinuses become cleansed and her soul rejuvenated. The warmth of the bright sun bathes her face and arms as she breaks through the forest. Soon, she removes her sweatshirt, tying it around her waist.

Sandy finds that the hill she is climbing isn't too steep and she makes it up to the top rather quickly and with little effort. In hopes of seeing another view of the ocean as she reaches the top, she is disappointed to find a meadow with tall grasses stretched out in front of her. She stops for a moment in disbelief.

This meadow before her is exactly like the beautiful meadow of her nightmare. She takes a minute to gather her wits about her. She thinks of the dream again, wondering what it means. The meadow grasses are bending slightly to the rhythm of wind. But here, there is no Andrew or evil dark-haired woman.

In the distance stands an old red barn. She continues towards the barn and up the rise. From atop the hill she turns to look behind her. Still feeling a little freaked out by the coincidence of the meadow she just walked through to the meadow of her dream, she pauses. The meadow and pine forest is below her and a stiff ocean breeze greets her, slapping her face and tussling her hair. Suddenly chilled, she decides to put on her sweatshirt once again.

From this direction she can see Andrew's cottage below and a vast and wild ocean behind and around it. In the opposite direction, she can even see the other side of the island and the ferry landing as well. She realizes that Andrew's property starts at his cottage and extends to the highest point of the island, which gives her a most splendid view of most of Owl's Nest. She relaxes as she takes in the views putting her thoughts of the dream away.

She remains transfixed for a few moments until her curiosity gets the best of her. She decides to explore the barn. Sandy wonders what treasures Andrew has stored in there. Perhaps she can unlock some of the mystery behind the man she once knew and wants to know better.

The worn wooden doors to the barn are huge and heavy. Over the years they had warped and became uneven. With great effort, Sandy manages to pull one of them open allowing sunlight to shine inside, illuminating the corners and crevices of the vast space.

Immediately inside the doors is a large tractor. She thinks that it must be used to mow the meadow. Leaning against the tractor is a giant snow blade. She quickly assumes it is used to plow the driveway during early fall snows, before Andrew leaves for the winter. She continues exploring as she moves around to the back of the mower.

It is somewhat darker behind the tractor as the large machine blocks the light. Sandy finds a few taped-up boxes, some primitive furniture covered in years of dust, and a motorcycle. To her untrained eye the motorcycle looks to be an older model and obviously rarely driven. It leans close to a larger piece of furniture that is carefully and meticulously covered by a large canvas cloth.

Squeezing her way between the motorcycle and the wrapped piece of furniture, Sandy gets a better look. The canvas covering is secured in place with bungee cords that are wrapped tightly around it. Whatever it is, great care was given it. Andrew intentionally made sure it was protected. No moisture, dirt or anything else could possibly get to it.

At this point in her exploration, Sandy looks around the barn. There isn't much else in the barn but a few bales of hay, some machinery and a bunch of tools hanging on the walls. Nothing else of interest peaks her curiosity except this massive package. She walks to the front doors feeling somewhat guilty for what she is about to do and looks out. Only ocean sounds and the beautiful meadow greet her.

Drawn back into the barn and to the covered piece of furniture, she unhooks the cords that wrap around the canvas. Once she removes all the cords, she lifts a corner of the canvas carefully as guilt once again overtakes her.

"Would Andrew mind that she is prying into his business? Would he be angry at her discovery?" She used to know Andrew well. Now, after all these years, she wasn't so sure. Pushing her doubts of Andrew and her fears aside, she peers underneath the canvas and sees what appears to be a large piece of mahogany wood. She realizes that unless she uncovers the whole piece, she will not be able to tell what it is. The wood is in perfect shape and appears to be shiny and polished. Sandy lifts the heavy canvas back further, eventually completely pulling it off.

She is amazed as she looks at what sits before her. Here in this dilapidated old dusty barn sits the most beautiful antique organ Sandy had ever seen. It is big. It is ornate and resembles organs that sit in large churches. The stool, in the same mahogany wood, is attached to what looks to be pedals and the rest of the organ.

Sandy is confused. Once again she thinks, "Do I know Andrew anymore?" She didn't remember that he played the organ or any instrument for that matter in college. All that he did in college was chase women as he worked haphazardly on a business degree.

He didn't appear to have an ounce of musical ability in him. She remembered that he rarely even listened to music at all. Surely, this wasn't his organ. Andrew as an organ player just does not fit his personality, she thinks. Still confused, Sandy decides that he must have inherited it from someone in his family. After coming up with that conclusion, she is satisfied.

Sandy begins to cover the beautiful organ back up again but then she sees an electrical cord coming out from behind the organ. It is plugged into an extension cord. She follows the extension cord across the floor of the barn to where she sees it is plugged into the electrical socket on the wall. This new discovery makes no sense. Someone must play this organ, she decides. Is it Andrew?

She walks quickly to the organ once again and pulls back the cover that is over the keys. She finds the switch and turns it on. The huge organ begins to hum. The hum gets louder and louder. Sandy sits on the bench and pushes down a key. Nothing happens. Then she remembers the bars and pushes some of them with her feet. Loud sounds begin to bleed from the organ. The sound astonishes her but she keeps on hitting the keys and moving her feet. It is not music. As she tries to remember the little bit of piano she once knew, she begins to hammer out a simple tune she played as a child.

While Sandy plays, Andrew and Toby leave the market with a bag of bagels and coffee creamer and jump back into the truck. Knowing that they only have one more day together, he is planning their day in his mind as he bumps along the road. Pulling up in front of the cottage, he turns off the ignition and hops out of the truck with Toby at his heels.

Even though the ocean sounds are loud, he hears something more. Toby and Andrew both look towards the meadow in the direction of the noise. Toby tilts his head and runs up the path to the meadow. Andrew sets the bag of groceries on the hood of his truck and chases behind his dog. The closer the two get to the barn, the louder and more distinct the sound is. Andrew knows it is the organ. He sees the barn door ajar and steps inside. Toby runs over to the organ and Sandy.

Surprised at Toby's presence, Sandy stops hitting the keys and turns around. Andrew is there in the doorway. Sandy has a hard time making out the look on his face with the sunlight at his back. She gets up and walks over to him and sees that his face is distorted in a way unnatural for him. She knows right then that he is not pleased with her.

"What are you doing in here, Sandy?" he asks.

"Well, I went for a walk this morning, seeing that you and Toby were gone, and I discovered the barn with this beautiful organ inside." She waits for his reaction.

"I can see that," he says.

"Is this organ yours? Do you play?" Sandy questions.

"I used to play a long time ago."

"When, in college?"

Andrew sits on a box then and pats the box next to him. "Okay... have a seat next to me and I will tell you."

"Yes," he tells her with hesitation, "I was a composition major at Boston Conservatory of Music before I met you and Jim at Boston College."

Sandy's mouth drops as he continues.

"I wrote organ and piano compositions. I have written many, many pieces of music."

"What?" Sandy questions. "How come Jim and I never knew? What happened to make you quit? Why did you give it all up, Andrew?"

Andrew answers slowly, "Hey, I know it may seem kinda stupid and shallow now, but music was my life then. It was more than a hobby or even a career for me...music filled every cell in my being. I know it sounds foolish now, but I defined myself by my love of music. I dreamed of how I could express myself to the world. My whole self esteem was tied up in who I was behind the keyboard."

Sandy almost saw Andrew slowly implode as he spoke.

"I can't believe this. How was it possible for you to cut out such a large piece of who you were? Jim and I never knew about this part of you."

Andrew hesitates a moment then continues, "When I went to the conservatory, it was all about how I could improve and how I could learn to do more. I found out, the hard way, that music is not **"life"** to everyone like it was to me. I was a big boy and was willing to take criticism, but my professors were all about form, and structure, and the mathematics of music. They had long since lost their love of music and it became a job to them. I never ever saw even one of them smile, or close their eyes as they listened, or much less cry when they heard something beautiful.

For my sophomore recital, I performed a piece that I had written... _When the Lord Dreams_. Maybe a little pompous for a teenager, but the song was more than just music to me; it was spiritual. It was the best I had ever written. OK...I know what you're thinking...yes, I was just a sophomore, but this piece was good. I know it was!

Nothing was said much after the recital, but I had learned not to expect much from my professors. I was called back into school three days later. I had been given a C- for the semester based primarily on my performance. I was furious and let my professor know how I felt.

It was pretty ugly. I was pretty ugly. Unfortunately, my professor did not like being talked down to, so he invited several of the other professors to review the tape of the recital. The group of five professors spent the next three hours critiquing my music, my style, and my abilities. Note for note, bar for bar, and movement by movement. They took turns trashing my finished assignment, and that is all it was to them. Just another assignment turned in by a young, dreamy eyed student.

Again, it may sound petty to you, but this piece was like a child to me. I conceived it; I nourished the idea, and raised it up from a few notes on my chart, to a fully developed child...and she was beautiful."

Andrew pauses, "I know, I know...too much information. Yeah...I uh, I am just embarrassing myself now."

With tears in her eyes, Sandy begs Andrew to go on.

"I know it sounds dumb, but my child was beautiful. She had personality, she had light, and she was mine. And they killed her. I have never felt so humiliated in all my life. I had laid out my soul to everyone, and they did not like what they saw. I had never wondered if I had talent before. I never wondered if I had the skills. As far as that goes, I never doubted the essence of who I was before. My love of music, along with _Dreams,_ had been killed...dead and buried, and I chose to leave it that way.

That is why I was that way in college. It is so easy to fill your life with nothing, if you have lost sight of who you are. I tried so hard to replace my love of music with women and sex. You and Jim were the one bright spots in my life. I would have been lost without the two of you."

Andrew looks down as if he had unloaded a massive weight and sighs, "The Andrew you know is really just a part of me...and maybe not the best part."

He sits quietly for a few minutes then gets up to cover up the organ.

"I am so sorry, Andrew. I don't know what to say. I have lost those who I loved, but I never lost a part of myself. Andrew... I am sorry; I did not really mean it that way. I just don't know how I would feel. I can't imagine making the decision to give up something that I loved... something that was so much a part of me."

Tying the straps around the tarps, Andrew replies, "I guess I never felt like I made a conscious decision, you know, to walk away. I just lost interest. If my best efforts were worthless, I was not really giving up on anything of value, you know. Anyway, it just was what it was."

"I don't know, Andrew. It just seems like such an enormous waste of talent. So you never played again...you never *wanted* to play again?" Sandy wanted to know.

"No, and I won't ever play again."

"But you must play your music up here in the barn sometimes. The organ is plugged in."

"Yes, I play for Toby, but that is it. Tobe loves my playing, but you know, he's a dog."

"Would you consider playing for me?" Sandy asks.

"I know that it is hard to understand, Sandy, but I just don't think I want to play for anyone again."

"You know," Sandy says in a quiet voice, "knowing this about you makes you even more special to me. Whether you ever play again or not, *I* will know that you have the heart of a musician...and that is special to me."

CHAPTER 18

Church Music

One evening after Mr. Night Janitor had gone home for the day, Beth opened the door at the top of the stairs leading out of the boiler room. Curious as to what was up the stairs she looked carefully in both directions and listened intently before proceeding into the long hallway. Tonight was the night she was to discover what lay beyond her sanctuary, her home.

Light spilled from beautiful lanterns that hung from an exceptionally tall ceiling. The metal work encasing the glass allowed the light to create geometric patterns that danced along the paneled walls.

She could see now that the long hallway was very ornate; massive throne-like oak chairs with cushions covered in unique needlepoint designs stood courtly on deep pile burgundy carpeting down the entire length of the hallway. It reminded Beth of a library until she saw the life-like oil paintings hanging on the walls.

Stately and proud looking priests or bishops, dressed in headgear and robes hung there as if in a gallery. Their names were boldly posted underneath. Each was mounted in an ornate gold frame with an attached small light that bathed the subjects in a soft glow. She counted fifteen of them lining the walls of the long hallway as she walked past. Bowing her head reverently to each portrait as she passed, she made her way slowly down the hall.

Turning to the right at the end of the hallway, she continued her walk. There were several closed doors on either side of this second hallway. She walked softly past them as to not make a sound. At the end of the second hallway stood ornately carved wooden doors. They had heavy metal rings for handles, and she wasn't sure how to open them.

Thinking she heard something, Beth looked behind her down the long hallway. There, on the other end, were the same styled wooden doors. She paused, searching for silence knowing that no one else should be in the church this late at night.

The gentle sound found her again. It was faint, but it was there. Feeling the door in front of her, she carefully leaned towards it and put her ear against the wood. Soft music came from behind the closed door. Unable to stop herself, Beth slowly and carefully pulled on the massive ring so that the wooden door would open just wide enough for her slight body to fit through.

As she slipped through the space, notes danced their way into her consciousness and she was hypnotized. Quite like the Pied Piper of England, Beth couldn't help but follow. She made her way quickly through a large room filled with dining tables and chairs. The music grew in intensity and splendor as she followed it through the massive stainless and sterile kitchen.

The door leading from the kitchen opened into a large vestibule. She knew then that she must be at the front of a sanctuary. Suddenly, memories of attending Mass with the sisters of St. Cecilia overshadowed the entrancing music. Beth hesitated, weighing the pain of her past against the beauty of the music. Not taking the time to give her memory credence, she hurried to the entry ahead of her. The doors to the sanctuary were closed, but the pleasing melody captured her like nothing else ever had. She allowed the sweet sounds to wash over her, permeating all of her senses.

Peaking through the yellow stained-glass window in the door, she realized she must be in a room behind the choir loft and in the front of the cathedral. Sitting at the massive organ was a man dressed in striped pants and a coat, the tails falling over the organ's stool. His hair was long, white, and disheveled looking. He moved his hands, feet, and body rapidly but in total unison with the music.

He was so focused on his playing that she knew nothing else in the world mattered to him at that moment. She stood in awe until he finished. She had no idea how long that was. When the stranger's organ became silent, he bent his head forward almost touching his forehead to the keys. His hands rested at his side. He sat quietly for several minutes.

Beth was afraid to breath. Tears flooded from her eyes. Did this man know that he ushered beauty from depths his soul...and from the depths of her soul as well? Did he know that he took her breath away? Was his breath taken away too?

As the minutes ticked by like hours, the man finally got up from the stool of the organ. He turned several knobs and then walked away from the organ and down a few stairs and was out of her sight. He must have headed towards the back of the sanctuary, she thought. She finally heard the loud thud of the door closing behind him. With that, she opened the door that she had stood behind.

She was now able to view a massive sanctuary. It was the most beautiful room Beth had ever seen. This cathedral was breathtaking. She had no idea that she was residing in such a beautiful place. It seemed fitting though, as she thought about it. Here she was back once again, in a Catholic building, a place of worship and adoration. Beth fell down on the wooden floor and wept. She wept for the music, for the man, and ultimately, for herself.

The next evening, Beth made her way slowly and quietly back to the sanctuary. She longed to hear the beautiful organ music again. As she closed the large wooden doors behind her, she was greeted with silence. She hurried through the dining room into the kitchen, through the vestibule, and finally to the sanctuary. It was dark. No lights, no music and no mystery man. She was disappointed.

Several weeks crept by with no music. Each evening she would venture up to the sanctuary, only to be disappointed once again. Finally, after all those weeks, he returned. Her heart beat against the wall of her chest as she approached her vantage point three weeks after first hearing his music. He was there, playing so masterfully once again. She looked around her, desperate to find a more comfortable place to listen to his music and most importantly to watch him play. Seeing a curved set of stairs in the corner of the vestibule, she followed them up and wound her way to a balcony that wrapped around the back of the sanctuary.

She crept to the front of the balcony in order to see well. The old wooden floor creaked beneath her feet as she crept, but she knew the sounds of the organ masked it. Finally, she could see the man and hear *and* feel his music. She was able to see the side of his face now. He appeared to be younger than she originally thought. With the dim light crossing his face and hair, she could see that his hair was not white at all, but blond. Perhaps he was only a few years older than her? He was magnificent. At that moment, with the organ music filling the church, Beth fell deeply in love with the man and his music.

She listened as she slowly sat down as low as possible on the floor, watching as his hands flew across the keys. He played the same music that he had the last time she heard him, but it seemed to her to be more complex, deeper and with even more feeling than he played with before. It was stunningly beautiful. *He* was beautiful. She didn't understand the feelings that surfaced from the core of her body. The music brought warmth to her soul and a happiness to her being. He played without stopping and with so much emotion that Beth couldn't take her eyes off him. Time had no meaning for her. Little did she know that time had no meaning for the organist either.

CHAPTER 19

"When the Lord Dreams"

Late into the evening, after Sandy had called it a night, Andrew laid in bed unable to sleep thinking of his music. She had discovered the organ this morning and she wanted him to play for her. Could he possibly open up to her and share his love of music, his love of the organ, and his raw emotions with her. Was it time to expose his heart with all its deep valleys and hidden truths?

He thought of that time so many years ago when he discovered that young teenage girl watching him practice in St. Mary's Cathedral. He had noticed her in the shadows. She was crouched down in the balcony. When he had stopped playing, she was bent over sobbing into the carpet. Her eyes were full of tears. Not out of fear or sadness, but out of joy and beauty. When he looked up and saw her, she ran away. As the door slammed behind her, she turned and shouted, "Your music is the most beautiful music I have ever heard! Thank you for playing for me!"

If a perfect stranger could love his arrangement of _When the Lord Dreams_ like she did, perhaps Sandy would too. But a lot had changed within his heart and soul since then. His music demanded his heart, his soul, _and_ his emotions. Was it time for his heart to be released after being locked away for so long? Would Sandy be able to feel all the sadness and sorrow in his heart if he played for her? Could he be vulnerable with her?

With fear chasing his thoughts, Andrew made up his mind.

He jumps out of his bed, and runs to Sandy's bedroom door and is about to knock when he decides against it. Instead, Andrew decides to go up to the barn and set everything up before he invites her to come and listen. Grabbing his coat and some matches, he runs up to the barn with Toby chasing him.

"I know it is one in the morning, Bud. I am sorry to wake you but I have something very important to do up here at the barn. Come on, boy."

Toby runs ahead of him now, towards the barn doors as if he knows exactly what Andrew is going to do. The moon is full and hangs low in the sky directly over the barn. Entering the building, Andrew goes to a big dusty trunk and opens it. He pulls out ten old oil lanterns and begins to light them with matches. He slides the cover off his organ and places the lanterns all around. He pulls a couple of hay bales over to the side of the organ for Sandy to sit on. Looking around, he decides that the scene is perfect.

Running back down the hill, Andrew plays with his best friend. Toby jumps and runs, loving the game that they are playing in the middle of the night. Once back down at the cottage, Andrew tiptoes into the kitchen and gets a nice bottle of wine out of the cabinet as well as two glasses. No, he suddenly changes his mind...we need something *special* to drink tonight. Andrew puts the wine bottle back in the cabinet and pulls out a bottle of champagne he had been saving. He didn't know what he was saving it for until tonight. He put the wine glasses back and got out the two champagne glasses and a bucket. He filled it with ice.

"Okay, Tobe, wish me luck...tonight is the night."

Knocking on Sandy's door, Andrew says to her, "Come up to the barn with me. I want to show you something."

Hearing the knock on her door, she sits up in bed and rubs her eyes, looking at the clock on the dresser. With a sense of panic she asks, "Is there something wrong? What's the matter? Are you alright?"

Andrew quickly assures her that everything is okay. "I'm just excited...I think." He's questioning his own motives at this point.

"Do you *know* what time it is?" Sandy says in mock frustration. "Oh, just come on in here Andrew Morgan."

He opens the door switching on the lamp on the dresser.

"Yes," he sheepishly answers. "I know it is late."

"Now, what did you say, Andrew?" She asks not sure that she had heard him correctly.

Sitting on the bed next to her, Andrew repeats, "Would you please come up to the barn with me. I think that I would like to play something for you...you know.... uhh, on that organ that I was never going to play again."

"Oh, *that* organ...of course, I will," Sandy beams.

Andrew bends forward and kisses her lips gently and says, "Come on then!"

CHAPTER 20

Renewed Confidence

Andrew and Sandy feel the excitement in the air as they stroll hand in hand up the pathway to the barn. Seeming to share their anticipation, the building is aglow with the lanterns' light painting the inside with romantic softness. The pale moonlight dances across the rooftop. Once inside the barn, Andrew sits her down gently on one of the bales of hay and places the champagne bucket and flutes on top of the organ.

With the soft glow of the lanterns surrounding them and the handsome man sitting at the organ in front of her, Sandy feels like she is a character in a romance novel. Smiling, she sits and watches him as he readies for his performance.

Andrew switches on the organ. Sitting very still and mustering up the courage he needs, he feels the beating of his heart. With fear biting at his confidence, he looks to Sandy. She shakes her head with encouragement and smiles at him as if to say, "Go ahead Andrew, play your heart out."

He turns back to the keyboard. Taking a long breath, Andrew begins to play. Slowly at first, making sure each note is played exactly and to its utmost perfection, he plays without emotion. He stops, his fingers freeze. His music is not right. Looking to Sandy for reassurance once again, he finds not only encouragement from her, but love. Her eyes are brimming over with love for him. At that moment he knows he loves her too. A deep passion for her begins to melt the lock to the hardened trap door of his heart. He gets up from the bench and walks over to her and sits down close to her. He holds her hands in his and looks deeply into her eyes.

"I love you, Sandy," he whispers. With those words spoken, the door to his heart is finally unlocked. He should have known that Sandy always held the key.

"I love you too, Andrew." Sandy says as a warmth runs deeply through her. Taking his face in her hands, she kisses him deeply.

With sudden tears in his eyes, and a renewed sense of confidence, Andrew gets off the hay bale and slowly walks over to the organ. Taking a seat on the bench once again, he begins to play. This time, his fingers fly effortlessly across the keys. The beautiful melody drifts throughout the barn and into the meadow. His music fills every crevice in the space and travels deep into his own heart continuing the healing process. As the music picks up its tempo, Andrew casts open the door to his heart forcing Beth to leave. His music mirrors the struggle he has with her as he forces his ex-wife to release him.

With Beth finally gone from deep within his heart, his music reaches a fever pitch and he knows freedom - the liberty now to allow love to reside once again in his lonely heart. He pours out all the pent-up raw emotions that he has harbored for years through his fingers into his composition. In return, love and happiness completely fill his entire being. Performing magnificently now, he continues to play his beautiful masterpiece, just for Sandy.

CHAPTER 21

The Lighthouse

Waking up on her last day on the island with Andrew, Sandy knows love. Their time together last night was beyond anything she had ever experienced. Her love for him overflowed as his music, his presence, and his love filled her.

Feeling alive for the first time since Jim's death, Sandy slips out of bed quietly, gets dressed and goes to the sea.

The haggard, rough and unruly shore, with its vast array of disarray, greets Sandy on her fourth morning on the island. Standing on the porch, she sips her coffee as she looks to the seashore. Rocks of every color, shape and size, and tide-shoveled driftwood piled in small heaps around the dead sea-grasses, create a masterpiece of its own. To her, it looks as if Mother Nature had thrown this odd mixture up into the sky and let it land where it may as she crafted Maine's unique coastline.

Messy is her first thought as she peers down from the porch above. "The shore here in Maine is messy." she says aloud.

"No." Sandy rethinks her statement. "This rocky beach is magnificent," she whispers, being suddenly awestruck by what she is witnessing from the porch of Andrew's cottage.

Appreciating the fact that this shoreline is nothing like the clean, white sandy beaches of Destin, the beaches she is most familiar with, Sandy embraces it. Nor is life here on Owl's Nest anything like her quiet, tedious one she is accustomed to back in Tennessee. She quickly decides that she will happily step out of her comfort zone to be here on this rugged coast of Maine with Andrew. Sandy has found love here, so *here* is where she shall stay.

Still hearing the sea and looking to the muddled beach below her, Sandy understands something important. This newly found love that she and Andrew have recently rekindled is very much like this messy but magnificent beach. Each heart was in shambles, unruly, and camouflaged, hiding truths and pain deep within. There is no doubt in her mind that she had to join Andrew here in Owl's Nest so they could each expose their hidden truths and tremendous pain in order to find each other again.

With the dark tan of the muddy sand, camouflaging the color palette of the disorderly shore, it is almost impossible to see what lies beneath. Normally, Sandy would choose to protect her feet, wearing shoes when walking along this shore. If she didn't she would most definitely receive a deep and nasty wound from the hazards lurking there. But today she chooses something different.

And normally, she would not venture out on this beach, due to the fear in her own heart of the uncertainty of its waters as well as the pain it might bring. But today, again, she chooses something different. Out of defiance to that unruly fear within her heart, she sits down on the swing and removes her socks and boots. Gingerly treading amongst the sharp rocks and sticks, she will navigate her way along this uncharted shore, facing her fears in an attempt to repair her brokenness.

Barefoot and with her heart exposed, she is ready to face her fears alone. She descends the safety of porch proceeding down the rickety steps to the shore. Cold on the outside, but with a steady - growing warmth inside, Sandy is glad she is here walking this unpredictable beach. The wildness of Maine, as well as the love she has found on this island is as exciting as it is raw.

She smiles and notes that the day is gray, with a bitter breeze blowing in from the water, but that doesn't deter her. The sea is angry and the birds seem to mimic its fury. Still, she chases her fears away and she remains euphoric. Sandy takes in some deep breaths feeling the air's freshness seep into her nostrils. It is a cleansing of sorts- a deep cleaning of her heart and mind.

Sandy's emotions are overflowing, jumping around from one thought to the next. She allows her mind to fill with nothingness except the scene around her. For the first time *ever* she can feel the beauty of the sea in her heart. As she slowly calms her mind to clear the cobwebs of her life, she feels a new sense of peace and tranquility settle in there. Feeling hopeful, she thinks that perhaps today is the day the water and she can stop their bickering and find peace. Is it conceivable that she could finally forgive the twelve-year old Sandy for Mary's death? And perhaps she will even forgive herself for falling for Andrew, while she was married to Jim, all those years ago. As she climbs amongst the rocks, wood and earth she is astonished with the renewed spring to her step as well as within her heart. She walks briskly now along the shore as she kicks at the water. The shroud of guilt that had covered her heart for all these years was finally lifting.

While absorbed in her thoughts, a giant shadow overtakes her. Sandy looks up to see a massive lighthouse directly in front of her. How had she walked so far down the beach in what seemed like a few minutes of time? She looks back to see Andrew's cottage around the bend, a speck on the shoreline. She wonders now if she should have left Andrew a note as to her whereabouts. But as quickly as that thought enters her mind, it vanishes because she feels the water lapping at her cold feet as the tide is coming in. Sandy realizes that she is on the spit of land where the lighthouse stands perched on giant boulders. She knows that if she is to remain safe from the waters, she has to find shelter in the lighthouse.

Quickly approaching the ancient monument, she revels at its details. How the sailors must have welcomed her light beaming from atop the lonely and majestic tower. Although abandoned for years, the electrified light there still remains a beacon to the ocean travelers along the rocky coast, even to this day.

Sandy makes her way climbing amongst the stacked and jagged boulders surrounding the lighthouse. Once up at the top of the jetty, she walks around the lighthouse looking for a door. She finds an old and peeling wooden door cracked open as if to say, "Please come in and take refuge."

She pulls at the metal handle and with difficulty slides the heavy door across the stone threshold. When she opens the door wide enough for her body to slip through the opening, she sees the massive stone steps before her. One step sits atop the next as they follow the curve of the massive post in the middle of the structure.

Sandy starts up the stairs ever so slowly inching her way upward. Tiny slits carved out of the stones along the outside wall greet her along the way, bringing the minimal light she needs to see. The climb is a long one.

At the top of the last stair a closed door greets her. She stretches high on her toes to grab at the handle of the door, but she cannot reach it. Taking her scarf from around her neck, she loops it though the ring of the handle to give her the leverage she needs to pull open the door. As she tugs on the scarf, she leans back with all her weight and balances on her toes. The additional space provided by the lean helps to free the door, but when that happens, Sandy flies outward away from the steps into the air. Falling, she loses her grip on the scarf and tumbles down the stone steps landing in a heap on the broader step a few feet below.

Stunned, Sandy sits on the cold stone step trying to remember what she was doing the minute before. She notices then that the back of her head is aching. She reaches around and feels wetness. She must have hit her head as she fell. She holds her hand over the wound hoping to stop the bleeding. Dizziness finds her now as she cups her heavy head in her hands.

After a few moments, as the dizziness leaves her, the pounding begins. Leaning against the sidewall of the tower she tries to focus on her problem. Confusion overtakes her. She searches around for something to stop the bleeding, and remembers her hat. She sees it several steps below her, and crawls down on her hands and knees to grab it. Sandy places it firmly on the wound and presses.

Dizziness overtakes her again, so she closes her eyes trying to steady her view. But her eyelids are heavy now and she gives in to the tiredness that envelops her as she sits. She falls deeply into an unwanted and dangerous sleep.

Andrew wakes up in his bed with a smile on his face. Tucking away his dreams from the night before, he reaches over to the other side of the bed to cuddle with Sandy. Realizing she is not there, he feels an uneasy sense of panic. Something isn't right. His smile disappears as he throws back the blankets, reaches for his moccasins and jumps from the bed. The morning air is crisp and foreboding.

He grabs his favorite sweatshirt out of the drawer. He chooses this particular sweatshirt because it is a constant reminder of the best seven years of his life. It is old and completely worn out, but wearing it has always given him a sense of calm. Snatching his baseball cap from the chair, he leaves the bedroom in search of Sandy.

Coffee is waiting for him. He searches the large room, but she is nowhere to be seen. He looks out to the porch expecting to see her. Stepping out on the porch, he pans the rocky shore, but still she is not there. Turning to go back inside, he sees Toby sleeping on the sofa. Toby would never be sleeping so soundly if he hadn't already made a trip around the evergreens for his morning constitutional. Looking at the clock on the wall Andrew realizes that Sandy must have been gone for hours. It was almost ten o'clock.

Opening the front door of the cottage, he sees that both cars remain. He yells for her then, hoping she is walking down the road. Andrew is met with silence. As he gulps down the remainder of his coffee, worry races into his thoughts. Although unlike her, he fears she must have gone for a walk down the beach. Andrew runs back to the porch to assess his worst suspicions. Her socks and boots are sitting beneath the swing. Water was lapping several of the cottage's steps now. The tide was in. Afraid she might be in danger, he grabs his coat from the hall tree and sees that hers is gone. Yelling for Toby, they run out the front door.

Andrew and Toby jump into the truck knowing that they would not be able to walk the beach at high tide. He is hoping to find her as he drives along the shore road surveying the coast. Deciding that Sandy would go towards the lighthouse, he heads in that direction.

He reaches the lighthouse within minutes and runs along the jetty with the wild ocean smacking the rocks below. He knows Sandy would go into the lighthouse if given a chance, so he pulls at the handle on the slightly ajar door in front of him.

"Sandy, are you up there?" Andrew screams, as he takes the stone steps two at a time. Around and around he goes, calling out to her as he makes his way to the top. The sea is violent with its angry roar and his voice gets lost in it. He is sure Sandy can't hear him if she is above him in the lighthouse. As he gets to the top, he sees her. She is slumped on a step just a few feet from the door at the top. Her head is resting in her hands.

He reaches out to take her hand and sits down beside her. She doesn't stir. He shakes her then and she squints up at him.

"What happened Sandy? Are you alright?" She doesn't answer.

He sees her bloodied hat in her hand and knows she is hurt. He examines her head and finds blood and red hair mingled together forming a scab on the back of her head. He asks her if she is able to make it up the few remaining stairs. That is when he sees her bare feet. "Why did you take your shoes off?" Once again, Sandy doesn't answer.

Andrew knows a sofa awaits them at the top. He looks towards the door and sees her wool scarf hanging from the ring handle on the door. He smiles imagining what she must have been trying to do. He pulls on her scarf, opening the door. Gently, he picks her up from the step and carries her up the remaining steps and through the door.

The glorious view overtakes both of them as they enter the small round room. Dizziness returns to her and she slumps against Andrews's body. He places her gently on the couch, and shifts the musty pillows under her head.

Stable once again, she smiles up at Andrew as he sits on the floor next to her head. He breaths deeply and begins to rubs her face. He takes his jacket off and places it over her lower body and ice cold feet. Her toes are a bright red and he begins to rub them to warm them up.

Sandy looks up trying to clear her head and says, "How did you know I was here?"

"I really don't know," Andrew says. "When I woke up this morning and you were not there, I guess I might have panicked. This old lighthouse was the only place that I could think that you might have gone. I was so relieved to see you...even if you were a bloodied mess and unconscious," he says, beginning a smile. He kisses her forehead and then her lips. She reaches up and places her cold hand on his cheek.

"We must get you warmer." Andrew says as he begins to pull off the sweatshirt he is wearing. Sandy stops him and reads aloud the words written in faded letters across his chest. "WORLD'S BEST DAD. Please tell me about Thad, Andrew, I want to know all about your son." Knowing that she needed to rest for a while before they attempted to leave, he starts telling Sandy about Thad.

"His full name was Thaddeus Andrew Morgan, but we called him Thad," Andrew says as his voice catches for a moment. "Thad was born after only seven months of marriage to my wife, Beth. He had my eyes and blonde hair, but Beth's dimples, height and beauty. He truly was a beautiful little boy. I was afraid to hold him at first. He was so tiny. I have photos at the cottage, if you want to see them."

Sandy looks to him, and smiles, knowing how very painful it must be for him to talk about his child. And how much he must still miss him. She too understood the horrific pain of losing someone so close. She thought about the photo of Thad that she had admired on Andrew's nightstand. He had to have been around two years old when the photo was taken. Andrew was lifting him up over his head, and both of them were laughing as they played. He had many photos of Thad scattered in frames around his bedroom and den. He *was* a beautiful little boy.

Andrew continues. "The doctor said it was a miracle that Beth was even able to carry the little guy for the seven months that she did. Her uterus and vagina had been previously damaged so badly that she wouldn't be able to have a natural delivery. So, the doctor delivered Thad early by C-section."

Sandy whispered in shock, "Oh no, what caused her body such damage?"

"Beth would never talk about it with me. But finally one day, I privately asked the doctor what he thought had happened to her in the past. I feared for our unborn child's safety. The doctor shared with me in confidence that he was sure that Beth would never be able to have another baby; that he saw evidence of a traumatic injury and lots of scar tissue from years before, probably when she was a teen. He assumed from what he saw that her young body had been ravaged by rape and was badly damaged. He said that it was truly a miracle that she conceived and had carried Thad for as long as she did. The doctor also told me that it was a miracle that Beth had survived such an ordeal."

Sandy gently squeezed his hand as she said, "Oh, my gosh. That poor woman. Did she ever tell you what had happened?"

"No, Beth would never talk about her past at all. I did know her mother had left her at an orphanage when she was young girl, but that is all she ever told me."

"I feel so sorry for her. Did she ever see a therapist about her past?"

"No, I tried to get her to go to one, when the gynecologist told me what he thought had happened to her, but Beth got angry with me for even mentioning it. She said that her past was no one's business, but her own. I dropped the subject with her.

Thad's baby years were just a blur for me, as I had to spend most of my time back then working. Beth had quit her job to stay home with Thad. Money was very tight. I wanted her to stay home, but as a result, I was gone most of every week traveling for my job. Thad was a good baby with a calm demeanor. I attribute that to me," Andrew laughed. He was quiet for a minute and then went on.

"Now, I wish I could have those early years back. When Thad was four and in preschool, I changed jobs. I hated missing out on those years when I couldn't be there for my son. With the new job, I did not have to travel and was able to have more time at home.

Even though the doctor suggested otherwise, we tried to get pregnant almost immediately after Thad's birth. Beth was relentless. I tried to discourage it knowing that probably she would never get pregnant again. Due to her persistence, we tried for four long years."

Andrew looks over at Sandy, and realizes that she might need some water. She was still looking pale. He remembered that he had a bottle of water out in the truck.

"Hold on, I'm going to run down and get you a bottle of water. Are you okay for a few minutes? I will be right back." He kisses her on the cheek and leaves her saying, "Don't get off this couch, you hear me, young lady."

"Okay, I'll be right here." Sandy says as she smiles up at him.

Andrew reaches the bottom of the lighthouse steps and stands on the jetty fixating on the rocky shore. His mind is brimming over with thoughts of Beth and Thad, but mostly of Sandy. It had been very healing to tell Sandy about Beth and Thad; things that he hadn't ever said aloud before to anyone. He was glad that they were having this conversation. Remembering how very empty and vacant his heart had been after Thad's death and after leaving Beth, he also remembered wondering if he could possibly love again.

He thought he knew what love was when he fell so hard for Beth that day in the snack room at work. She was beautiful, fun loving, full of energy, much like Sandy. He fell for her the moment they officially met. Beth filled his empty, lifeless heart then, the heart that never thought he could have a meaningful relationship with a woman...that skirt-chasing selfish guy.

But Beth...she alone changed him.

He had become consumed with her. He wanted nothing but to make her happy. And he loved her with his whole heart. She loved him too for a while. But he soon found out that her love, unlike his, was a twisted wreckage of selfish ambition and obsession. She loved him for what he could give her. Not for his love, but his attention, his manhood, his body, his flesh.

To Beth, he was nothing more than an attractive man that could hold her, and make her pain go away, at least temporarily. His was a physical presence for her and she needed that desperately. She had so much pain in her heart that it was full. There was no room in her heart for anything else, especially Andrew.

He had always believed that deep down inside, she had wanted to trade the pain for love, but she had just never been able to make the transition. Instead, he had become nothing more than a personal band aide of sorts. He remembered trying to help her, but her pain remained un-named. Or was it the pain with many names? She would only tell him that it was an ache that she endured for most of her life, that he could not, nor would not, ever understand.

He knew it to be the pain of abandonment, the pain of not having a mother, the pain of loneliness. That pain that she held on to for their entire marriage seeped deep into her heart and had built an impenetrable fortress there. Beth *could not* love because she had never known love.

But here he was with Sandy in his favorite place in the entire world, and he *had been able to find* love once again. And Sandy was different than Beth in so many ways. Even though Sandy held the pain of losing her sister and Jim to tragic deaths, she was able to push the pain aside and invite him in. Andrew knew that after last night he had also changed. He was finally able to thrust Beth from his heart.

Leaving his thoughts of Beth behind, replacing them with thoughts of Sandy, he realizes that he hadn't gotten the water yet. He runs over to the truck to find the water in the cup holder and Toby still in the front seat waiting patiently.

"Oh Tobe, come on old boy. Sorry to keep you waiting all this time!"

Toby jumps from the truck and, as always, races ahead of him. Once inside the lighthouse, the two leap up the steps to Sandy. She is standing, wearing Andrew's jacket and looking out the window of the lighthouse.

He approaches her and puts his arms around her waist and kisses her on the neck. Toby jumps up on the couch and rolls on his back posturing himself for a "belly rub". Sandy turns and laughs at Toby. When she smiles, Andrew sees that special look in her eyes and then knows that he will never be without her again.

"Why don't you drink this bottle of water before we go back down the stairs." Andrew tells her.

"Sure." Sandy answers and the two of them sit down again on the couch with Toby.

"Will you finish telling me about Beth and Thad?" she says as she begins to rub Toby's chest.

"Yes, but only after I tell you that I love you." He kisses her gently. "*And,* you must drink this entire bottle of water." Sandy smiles, takes a sip of the water, and lies back to enjoy Andrew's voice...the voice of the man she loves.

He continues softly, "During those years after Thad was born, Beth became obsessed with having another child. She went through fertility treatments, but to no avail. She miscarried twice during those years, and it had been torturous to her fragile body.

One day, the doctor, out of concern for Beth's well being, both mentally and physically, finally got through to her. He told her that her uterus was not ever going to hold another fetus. She had tried long enough. I tried to reassure her that Thad was perfect. He was all I ever wanted or needed. But from then on, it was like she had built a wall around herself and Thad. I wasn't allowed in. I was banished to live on the outside; unable to unlock the door in the wall or to her heart."

Her obsession changed from pregnancy to motherhood. She paid me little attention. I was useless to her now...I couldn't provide the child she craved. She even took up sleeping in Thad's room on a twin bed. Her interest in life seeped out of her like water from a cracked vessel, slowly leaking out over time and leaving nothing but emptiness inside. She was quiet and depressed and rarely smiled, even when she played with Thad. We did our best to cheer her up. I took over much of his care then. She was unable, spending hours during the day in bed.

Thad did well in school and we signed up for all the sports...t-ball, soccer, kung Fu...I coached most of them. I cherish those times we had together. Over the course of three years, Beth moved her obsession to adoption. I think it was because she didn't feel Thad needed her as much any more. He was growing up and becoming more independent. She loved Thad with all the love she had, but she wanted and needed more. All she seemed to dwell upon was adopting a child. It filled her every thought from morning until night.

She joined a church on her own, not including Thad or me. She attended that church every time the doors were open. She began going on mission trips around the world with her church. She would be gone for weeks at a time, leaving us to fend for ourselves. She only returned home to plan and repack for her next trip. She desperately wanted and needed to help the orphans. I thought that perhaps it was her way of giving back since she so fully understood the orphans' plight.

I did think it a noble calling on one hand, but I wasn't sold on the idea of adoption on the other. I began to see a flicker of happiness in her so I supported her trips. I had hoped they would bring her back to us. However, Beth's obsession with adoption seemed to grow with each mission trip she went on.

She had been distant before she left on her fourth mission trip. Then on that last trip, she arrived at the baggage claim with a child in her arms. It was a baby girl from China. This happened just a couple of weeks before Thad's death."

"Was that the baby girl I saw in Beth's arms at Thad's funeral?" Sandy asked.

"Yes." Andrew answered.

"Several months after Thad's death, the stress, the loneliness, and the complete sadness of being married to Beth became too much for me. Beth had been so focused on her adopted baby girl that she could not be with me, never even talking to me for more than a few minutes of time.

She never wanted to talk about Thad. It was like he never even existed in her mind. She continued sleeping in the baby's room on the single bed. I allowed her this little bit of comfort for a while, thinking that if this is what she needed to come back to me, then I would allow it. But time went by and nothing improved.

This new baby from China became her new obsession. I remember seeing a pamphlet from an adoption agency in Mexico on her desk and I knew I had to talk to her. I felt that she was having a difficult time accepting Thad's death and was trying to fill it with more children.

I desperately needed to talk about Thad with her. And I wanted to talk about the little girl that Beth had adopted, and most importantly about our deteriorating marriage. I felt at that point that I was left with a shadow of my wife.

I asked Beth to come into the living room and sit down with me for just a minute so we could talk. She agreed and sat down with the baby cuddled in her arms. I poured out my heart to her telling her of my concerns, my sadness over losing Thad, and how much I needed her to be present with me. I gently tried to explain to her that I wasn't ready for a baby so soon after our son's death."

Tears fill Andrew's eyes as he tells Sandy his story for the first time. His tears release his pent up pain, finally allowing it to escape from deep inside. Holding his hands, Sandy's caring look gives him permission to cry.

Continuing, because he has to get the rest of the story out, he cries, "I told her that I needed her and still loved her, but that she had become so distant since Thad's death. She just sat there tending to *her* little baby and didn't even respond. Can you believe that? She just sat on the couch looking straight ahead, ignoring me. I couldn't believe that she didn't care. I begged her to say something - anything. But still, I was greeted with silence. That's when I stopped talking. As I opened my heart to hers, I realized that once again she had already closed her heart to mine.

I could see in those vacant emerald green eyes of hers that she had no feelings left in her heart for me. That she had pushed me out when she brought the new baby in. And the strange thing is I could read a weird emptiness in her eyes. Behind her once mesmerizing emerald green eyes, there was a heart of stone.

I knew then that Beth was gone. She just wasn't there anymore. The woman I had fallen in love with, the mother of my deceased child, was gone. She sat there on the couch next to me without a sign of understanding or feelings. The only place her eyes would look, were at my lips as I formed my words. There was no emotion on her face at all. There was no question in my mind how she felt.

Then I just waited. I waited for something from her - a response of some kind. But, she just sat without speaking, remaining there, without looking at me, just *through me*. When the silence of the room finally overwhelmed me, I turned from her, took one last long look at my wife and left. I never saw her again.

I turned away from it all – *EVERYTHING*. The only solution I could come up with for my brokenness was to leave. Wanting to get as far away as possible from Beth, I got into my car and drove. I drove for fifteen hours straight only stopping for coffee and the bathroom.

Finally, when tiredness completely took over my body and mind, I stopped. It was in Clifton Forge, Virginia, that I found a small motel. I slept for an entire twenty-four hours. When I woke, I was still fully dressed. Washing my face, I returned to the bed and simply sat there staring at the empty wall of a grimy motel room. I knew that I could give up right then, or I could decide what I needed to do next. I had a good job in Nashville and didn't want to give it up, but I knew my marriage to Beth was over. As two days and nights turned into three, I finally made the decision to pick up the pieces of my life.

Leaving the motel and my job behind, I drove up the East coast as far as I could go…to Maine…searching for a quiet forgotten place, where Beth would never be able to find me. Somehow I stumbled upon Owl's Nest. Here, in the first few weeks of my life without Beth and Thad, I bought my cottage."

Whining on cue, Toby stirs and reaches his paw out placing it on Andrew's knee.

"Yes, Tobe, I met you here, didn't I ole boy? And you pretty much saved me at the same time that I was saving you." Andrew scratches his head roughly as he continues.

"Getting over the loss of Thad was so much harder than getting over the loss of my marriage to Beth. I can still see his face on that last day that I sent my little boy off to school. His backpack was securely fastened to his back, his lunch box in hand, and my kiss planted firmly on his forehead. I can see him now, turning and waving bye to me as he ran down the front walkway to his carpool that was waiting for him at the sidewalk. That was the last time I saw his smile, and the last time I smiled for a very long time."

Sandy grabbed Andrew's hands in hers and they both wept.

"I am so sorry, Andrew. I can't imagine how hard it must have been for you. I do know what it feels like to lose someone you love. I wish I could have been there for you back then. But, Andrew, I am here now."

CHAPTER 22

The Proposal

Sandy was scheduled to leave Owl's Nest the next morning. She had gone through quite an ordeal earlier that same day with her head injury. Andrew had taken her to the only clinic on the island, and the doctor had told them that she had suffered a concussion. Thankfully, it was a mild one. He put in a few stiches, and bandaged her head sending them home to rest for the remainder of the day.

Sandy felt awful that the two of them couldn't enjoy traipsing around the island for one last day. Andrew was fine spending time with her in the cottage. In fact, it ended up being the best plan for him.

For lunch, he made his famous chili and cornbread using his mom's recipes. Andrew told Sandy that she was not to move from the sofa as he cooked. They ate sitting on the sofa in front of the fire. He was pleased to see her appetite was as hearty as ever.

Earlier in the morning at the lighthouse, after Andrew had shared his gut-wrenching story of the loss of Thad and Beth, Andrew decided that he no longer wanted to live without Sandy. She made his life complete. He made up his mind that he wanted to spend the rest of his life with her. When they finally got back to the cottage, Andrew picked a single pink rose from his garden to give to Sandy when he would get down on one knee to ask her to be his wife. He didn't have a ring because his spontaneous decision left him no time to buy one. In his mind there was no time to waste as he had been without her and her love for too long already. After their late lunch, he had planned to kneel before her in front of the fire. But after he finished washing the dishes he saw that Sandy had gone out to the porch to watch the sunset. She sat on the porch swing and looked to the sea. It was raining over the water. She asked him to come out to watch the approaching rainstorm with her. He told her that he would be right there.

Grabbing the rose out of the refrigerator, Andrew stuffs it into his pocket as he joins Sandy on the porch. As he sits down on the swing next to her, she links her arm in his. Together, they watch the clouds and blowing rain approach. It is quite beautiful. The rain makes its way to the porch spraying both of their faces.

Pondering her words carefully, Sandy finally says, "Andrew, I feel as if this rain is rinsing away all the years of guilt and pain that we both have endured. I think love and happiness can come home now."

Knowing her words opened up the opportunity that he was waiting for, Andrew turns and kisses her saying, "Sandy, I love you." He gets down off the swing and kneels before her. "I want to spend the rest of my life with you. Please say you will marry me," and he hands her the smashed pink rose from his pocket.

Laughing sweetly at the site of the rose, Sandy answers softly, "Yes, of course, yes. I would love to spend the rest of my life with you Andrew Morgan...but only if we can live here filling this cottage with lots of babies."

Andrew laughs. "Of course, we can...I would love to have babies with you."

They kiss as the rain continues to fall, cleansing their hearts, and leaving a clear vision of what their future would be.

PART TWO

(Three Years Later)

CHAPTER 23

A New Islander

Margaret Buchannan arrives on Owl's Nest with renewed hope. She is in hopes of finding a nanny's job with that perfect family that she envisions. And she is anxious to get on with her life.

Setting her suitcases down by her feet, Margaret lifts the heavy brass knocker on the front door of the guesthouse and allows it to slam down on the door several times. She stands and waits. Finally the heavy door opens wide and a small elderly woman is standing there. Margaret introduces herself to the woman assuming she is the proprietor.

"Hi, I am Margaret Buchannan. I called last week."

"Hello Margaret. I am Delores. And that is what you can call me." She laughs like her name is a joke. "How was your trip? I hope the ride over on the ferry was okay. Sometimes, the sea can be rather rough this time of year."

She continues, "August is our 'tweener month where fall knocks on the door of summer and wants in. Sometimes, summer succumbs to autumn allowing him to seduce her. But when she does, the sea is like an angry husband and is unforgiving. I hope that isn't what you experienced today on the ferry, dear."

Margaret smiles, understanding her analogy well.

"Oh no, I had a fine trip over on the ferry. The water was very calm today. Thank you."

"I have prepared your room. I hope you will find it comfortable."

The two women walk into the front hallway of the grand house.

Margaret had wanted to find a motel to stay in while she was in

Owl's Nest since her finances were in short order. But upon researching, she found out that there were no motels or hotels on the island. There were only a handful of Inns and B&B's. She chose this one because the ad said that it was quiet, historic, and had a forlorn story of love lost in its history. She was sure most of the others had a story too, but she liked this story because it reminded her of her own. And when she called the proprietor, she was thrilled to find out that a vacant room was available.

Following the lady up the staircase, Margaret looks around and is happy with what she sees. The innkeeper walks ahead of her leading the way. She unlocks the door to Margaret's room and hands her the key. Margaret says, "This is quite lovely and I'm looking forward to my stay here." She continues to scan the room taking in the lovely decor.

Delores answers, "I am glad that you like the room. I know you said that you were not sure exactly how long you would be here, dear. Do you have any idea?"

"I don't know. If I can find work, I will stay indefinitely. But if not, I will have to go back to the mainland within a week."

"What kind of work are you looking for?"

"I am looking for a…. a nanny job, preferably with a younger child. If you know of anyone that is looking for one, I would be much obliged."

Because Delores knew most everyone on the island, and because Margaret looked to be a very straight-laced conservative young woman, the innkeeper responds, "I will keep my ears open." She realizes that her guest would stay at the inn a bit longer if she could find her a job, so she decides to investigate the options for her the next day.

"I will leave you now, other guests will be arriving later on, and I need to tidy their rooms. I hope you have a nice stay on our little island, Margaret. If you need anything, please come down to the front desk in the lobby and ring the bell there on the desk. My quarters are close by. Oh, and dinner will be served at six."

Like Delores said, dinner *was* served promptly at six o'clock. Margaret and the owners were the only diners that first evening. The meal that Delores prepared was one of the best home-cooked dinners that she had eaten in recent history. The seasoned cook served beef stroganoff over rice with rich brown gravy covering it all. There were bowls of fresh peas, julienne carrots, and a basket of homemade bread. Everything was served on fine china accompanied by sterling silverware. Margaret piled her plate high and ate every bite.

Following the delectable dinner, Delores served steaming apple pie with a slice of Vermont cheddar cheese on top. At first Margaret declined the cheddar on top of her pie but Delores insisted saying, "Oh child, everyone in Maine loves a bit of cheddar on homemade apple pie. You must try it." So Margaret did, and instantly she fell into Delores' good graces as well as finding a delicious new way to eat apple pie. With her hopes high and her stomach full, Margaret slept better that night than she had in quite some time.

At breakfast the next morning, Margaret sat next to a gentleman named Ernesto who had just arrived on the island from Europe. He was tall, dashing and quite attentive to her. She especially enjoyed the easy conversation she had with him.

When he found out that she was there alone, he asked if she had any interest in accompanying him on a tour of the island. He too was alone, had a car, and said he would love the company of a beautiful woman such as herself.

Since she was very anxious to explore the island, and she didn't have a car, she accepted Ernesto's invitation. Exploring the island with him in his convertible proved to be a most wonderful afternoon. Margaret actually allowed herself to have fun with him. She realized that it had been quite some time since she had enjoyed the company of a man.

He was attractive and entertaining. With neither of them knowing the island, they crisscrossed it several times driving down what seemed to be every road on the island. Margaret took a special interest in each detail and registered it in her mind. She commented to Ernesto that she loved driving on the untraveled roads best.

They drove to a lovely lighthouse that was the only tourist attraction on the island, and saw and photographed picturesque inns and grand houses that sat proudly on the bluffs overlooking the ocean. They shopped in all the small stores. She especially enjoyed walking down the roads arm and arm with Ernesto enjoying the colorful quint cottages with their lovely gardens.

They both delighted in their late lunch at the lobster shack, sitting together on a picnic table and sharing a lobster pot. Ernesto was a very interesting man and she was quite taken with him by the end of their afternoon together. Margaret knew that he could complicate things for her and she didn't need any complications in her life right now, so when they returned to the Inn in the early evening, she slipped away from him to her room.

That evening, at yet another scrumptious dinner of local cod, Delores slipped a note to Margaret with a phone number and name on it. Then she said, "I was in the grocery this morning and ran into a friend. I asked her if she knew anyone that could help you with a job. She mentioned a family, who I know well, that might be looking for a nanny. The husband travels a lot and his wife is pregnant with their second child. I think you should give her a call. Her name is Sandy Morgan. I think her child should be around 2 years old. She is about your age and I really think the two of you would get along well." Being extremely appreciative, Margaret thanked Delores for her help and slipped the note into her pocket. Excited for the possibility of the job, Margaret planned to call Sandy early the next morning.

Once again, Ernesto was most attentive to Margaret during dinner. He flirted with her, like most European men do, telling her how beautiful and desirable she was. When dinner was over, he invited her to stay downstairs with him. He asked her to sit with him in the somewhat private den where there was a cozy fireplace. He wanted to share a bottle of wine that he had picked up at the market on their afternoon jaunt.

Feeling pleased with herself and in the mood to celebrate the possibility of her new job, Margaret found herself saying "yes" to Ernesto. They sat together on the small couch next to a blazing fire. They talked about his failed marriages, his life, and businesses in Spain and elsewhere abroad. He told her that he lived in the beautiful city of Barcelona and would love to show her his home someday. Margaret enjoyed all his stories and allowed her mind to daydream about accompanying him to

Spain. The evening with Ernesto allowed her time to escape her reality for just a little while.

Never wanting to talk about herself much, she continued to transition the conversation back to him. He was quite enthralled with himself so redirecting him was never a problem. She only mentioned two noteworthy things about herself to Ernesto. She explained to him about the possibility of a job that she might get on the island. And that she was going through a nasty divorce and needed some time away. Ernesto said he understood her plight, as he was here to get away as well.

After they finished the bottle of white wine, she allowed his attentions to morph into more. Finding the den a little too public, as the owner continued to come in asking if they needed anything, Ernesto asked if she would accompany him on a walk along the shore. He goes on to say that the evening is a star-studded one, and he wants to spend just a bit more time with her.

"How can we ignore the beauty at our doorstep, it is simply enchanting, like you. Please join me Margaret. I would be forever grateful." And he kisses her hand as he gently pulls her from the sofa. The two spend the next several hours walking hand in hand along the shore teasing each other with kisses and attention. It was a magical night.

Long after midnight when Margaret finally says good night to Ernesto at the door of her room, she kisses him passionately. "You are a most beautiful woman, Margaret. Your magical eyes capture me and I don't want to let you go. Will I see you in the morning?" Ernesto pleads as he holds her hands in his and looks seductively into her eyes.

Without answering, Margaret turns from him, drops her shawl on the floor, leaving her bedroom door slightly ajar. Like the autumn winds that knock at the door of summer, Ernesto eagerly accepts her invitation and surrenders to Margaret's every need that evening.

As if a jealous husband, the sea grows wild and angry beating the shore relentlessly outside her bedroom window.

CHAPTER 24

New Career, New Life

Sandy pulls out the dishes and silverware from the kitchen cabinet and places them on the picnic table out on the almost completed deck. It is a warmer than usual day for this time of year in Owl's Nest, with a cerulean sky - a perfect day for lunch on the deck.

Andrew would be home in a few weeks from his successful summer European tour and Sandy is beside herself with excitement. She had missed him more than usual. She planned on talking to him when he returned home about slowing his schedule down some, especially now that the baby would be arriving in November. She knew he didn't want to be away from his family, but it had been necessary this summer due to the recent popularity of his music.

His soundtrack for this spring's blockbuster film "Into the Night" came out earlier in the year. With that and the two albums he had released over the last eighteen months, his successful music career made it possible for her to stay at home with Stephen. She was so proud of Andrew and his music. He had worked hard.

Four months had been a very long time to be away from him. Her body had changed greatly since he left, especially her belly. Stephen had started running around and had lost most of his baby fat. She hoped Andrew would recognize them both. Laughing aloud at the thought, Sandy continues to get ready for lunch.

Last year, she and Stephen traveled with Andrew, but it was difficult. Stephen needed to be in a stable environment and the constant traveling wore all three of them out. She finally decided to stay home in the cottage in Owl's Nest, waiting for Andrew when he could arrange time home. She knew that this year would be a busy one for him, but she supported him in every way possible.

With Andrew's concert schedule so demanding, Sandy decided to hire a nanny to help her with Stephen. Stephen was a good two-year old but he was very a very active child, and wore her out by the end of most days.

The constant bending over and lifting him was more tiring now that her belly was growing. Sandy was looking for someone to work about three days a week to watch over Stephen so that she could run errands and have time to rest. Andrew wholeheartedly supported her decision, wanting nothing but her comfort and good health. She went about the business of hiring the nanny.

Sandy had asked around town for the names of any women that might be interested in a nanny's job. It seemed that no one knew of anyone until she mentioned it to Sue when she ran into her while looking in the produce section at Stanton's Grocery store that morning.

Sue's face brightened when she told Sandy that in fact, she knew of someone who just might be interested. She told her about the woman who was staying with Delores. Delores had told her just that morning about her.

Sue goes on to say, "Delores said that this woman seemed sweet and straight-laced and in an urgent need of a job. Her name is Margaret Buchanan. She had recently moved to the island, according to Delores, after a traumatic divorce." Talking nonstop in the produce section as she made funny faces at Stephen, Sue told Sandy that she thought it would be a wonderful idea for Sandy to hire her since both women could use the help and companionship. Sandy smiled knowing that Sue always gave her opinion even if you really didn't ask for it.

Sue went on, "I just know the two of you would hit it off if you gave it a chance. And I bet you would become fast friends. Think about it dear. I must run, I have mountains of laundry at home that need to be hung out to dry and we all know that Samuel won't even think of doing it while I am gone." She laughed and kissed Stephen on the forehead as she waved good-bye.

"Thank you, Sue. I knew when I saw you here that you might know of someone. I shall get in touch with Delores then. Have fun hanging your laundry."

Sandy finished her shopping as she seriously considered the possibility of meeting Margaret. She would meet her mainly because Sandy adored Sue, just as Andrew did. And she knew that Sue had a way of knowing people down to their soul. She trusted Sue's gut instinct.

The strange thing was that when Sandy got back to the cottage after shopping that morning, her cell phone rang and the lady on the other end of the line said that she was Margaret Buchannan and that she had heard that she might be looking for a nanny. After chatting with Margaret for a few minutes on the phone, Sandy asked her to come over for an interview. Perhaps it was fate or just being at the right place at the right time, but Sandy believed their meeting was meant to be.

CHAPTER 25

Fast Friends

The next afternoon, Margaret Buchanan sat across from Sandy at the kitchen table of the cottage. She looked relaxed but professional in her stark white collared blouse and black pencil skirt that came just to her knee. She wore black flats and sat with her ankles crossed and her hands in her lap. She wore her hair up in a low bun with her short bangs pushed slightly to the side.

Margaret talked of her Christian background growing up in a strict Catholic family with parents that insisted that she and her seven brothers attend the Catholic school in their neighborhood. The school came complete with ruler toting and knuckle rapping nuns. She smiled as she spoke, which made her even more beautiful. She answered each question professionally and in such a caring way that Sandy was taken with her from the start. Even though Sandy imagined that she would hire a more matronly woman, she was surprised that she liked Margaret's easy manner and personality so much.

The only time Margaret wore a look of sadness on her face was when she mentioned that she had no children of her own and that she was going through a tumultuous divorce. She had come to Owl's Nest in hopes of getting a new start.

After the two-hour session, Sandy knew she had found the right woman for the job. Not only did she like her, but Stephen seemed taken with her too. He played with her and enjoyed the undivided attention that the woman gave him.

Over the first few weeks of Margaret's employment, she and Sandy

Morgan did become fast friends just as Sue had predicted. Margaret was an answer to prayer for Sandy for several reasons. Now that Margaret was doing most of the chores around the cottage and all of the food preparation, Sandy was able to rest if needed and focus on playing with Stephen. And almost as importantly, she really liked her.

The two women formed a comfortable relationship; one that seemed familiar. It was like they had been high school friends that had just now reconnected, and picked up right where they left off years before. It was amazing how fast their friendship grew and how much Sandy truly enjoyed being with Margaret. Sandy had been lonely and missing Andrew and Margaret filled the void to some degree. There weren't many younger women on the island, except the tourists, so Sandy had her over for dinner on many nights simply to enjoy her company.

The women would giggle and talk together after putting Stephen to bed until all hours of the night. Sometimes, Margaret would even spend the night in Stephen's room sleeping on the twin bed. Sandy was looking forward to Andrew's meeting her. She knew he would like her.

CHAPTER 26

Wedding Memories

Since Stephen was still taking his morning nap and Margaret hadn't arrived for the day, Sandy sat on the picnic bench thinking about her marriage to Andrew. It had been perfect. *He* was perfect. He loved her endlessly and she couldn't be happier. It seemed life had turned for the better for both of them from the day their eyes met on the banks of the ferry landing almost four years ago now.

Their engagement was extremely short, only lasting seven months, barely long enough to plan a wedding. And almost from the moment they reconnected, they both knew they would be married. Andrew seemed more fulfilled than ever now that he had found his music again. He was able to touch the world with his talents. Life was good. Sandy marveled at how happy she was living year round in Owl's Nest in Andrew's cottage. Their life together couldn't be more perfect.

The wedding had been simple, yet so very special to her, to Andrew, and in fact, to everyone that was in attendance. They married in a small church, which sat on a bluff overlooking the sea. A hundred years before, the church had been a tavern where all the fishermen came, after days on the sea, to drink and celebrate their homecoming. It was quaint and screamed of Maine's past. Andrew insisted on having the wedding there. They had both written their vows and Sandy could almost recite every beautiful word Andrew said to her that day.

The day of their wedding was splendid. The sky was even a darker blue than normal and the ocean was glass. Sandy thought of her simple pink wedding gown that flowed gently around her legs and dragged behind her along the worn wooden floor of the ancient church. She wore a crown of pink roses and baby's breath atop her hair. Her mother had loosely braided her curly locks and placed baby's breath within the plats. It was old-fashioned, just the way she wanted. Sandy wore her favorite color, pink. Most color analysts would have balked at the fact that she wore that color since her red hair, and blue eyes didn't blend with pink all that well. She didn't care, the significance of that color was far too important to her.

Andrew had surprised her the day of their wedding by filling the church with her favorite flower. He had collected hundreds of roses in every conceivable shade of pink that he could find from Sue and Samuel's garden...and from every other garden around the island.

Pink roses became her favorite for two very important reasons. The first reason was that Andrew had presented her with a smashed single pink rose on the day that he asked her to marry him. The second reason was that he had wanted to bring her a single pink rose to the ferry landing, on the day of their first meeting, but didn't. He had told her that he regretted that decision ever since.

Since the day he fell in love with her, Andrew presented her often with pink roses. Her eyes wandered to the kitchen table where she had placed a vase of pink roses that she had picked just this morning for Andrew.

Her mother and father and Andrew's parents had come to Owl's nest for the wedding. All of the other guests were locals. She and Andrew joked that the fish and lobster of the sea were given a holiday on their wedding day because all the fishermen were in attendance.

Since they both had been married before, this was to be a very small and intimate affair. It was intimate, but not small. Even though some of the locals didn't get a formal invitation, the whole town of Owl's Nest showed up at the wedding to help them celebrate. It was such a testament to their love for Andrew.

The reception was in Sue and Samuel's lovely garden. The fragrance of the colorful flowers drifted through the ceremony and reception all afternoon. All the women of the town lovingly prepared a feast of lobster chowder, fish, muscles and steaming bowls full of fresh vegetables from their gardens. The local bakery crafted the beautiful three-tiered wedding cake. Pink roses decorated the top layer and cascaded in a swirl down the side.

The music she and Andrew chose was from some of their favorite bands-old standards that were loved by all, so perfect for such a gathering in such a nostalgic place. Porter, Gershwin and Miller compositions set the tone for a romantic and timeless afternoon. The party was the talk of the town for several months afterwards. Even several new romances were hatched on that special day.

Their honeymoon was spent in Andrew's cottage by the sea. Andrew fashioned a sign out of an old piece of timber he found up in the barn and stood it up by the front door to the cottage. It read in very primitive handwriting, "Go away! Andrew and Sandy are enjoying each other's company and don't want visitors. You are welcome to come back in a week. Thank you kindly." Giggling again about his sign, Sandy decides right then that after lunch, she will go up to the barn, pull that sign out and place it once again by the front door for Andrew's homecoming.

As Sandy's thoughts drift to the honeymoon, Sandy hears the chugging of old Mr. Winter's car as he and Margaret drive up slowly to the front door of the cottage.

Margaret hops from the car and Sandy hears her thank Mr. Winter for the ride as she kisses him on the cheek. He is always such a dear to drive her to work each day, since she didn't have a car. Even though Sandy believes he does it mostly because he is 'sweet' on Margaret and simply wants to spend more time with her lovely, beautiful nanny. Although his wife, Mrs. Winter may think otherwise.

Seeing Sandy sitting on the bench on the deck, Mr. Winter turns off the engine and slowly gets out. Wearing his usual overalls, and fishing hat, he shuffles as fast as an eighty-five year old man can. He holds a big iron pot by the handle and walks over to the deck where Sandy is sitting. Margaret skips into the cottage's front door.

"Here you go, Ms. Sandy," he says as he hands her the steaming hot pot. "Mrs. Winter made you some good ole chowda' full of lobsta' and

clams and vegetables. It's good for you and for that little tike in there."
He pats her extended belly and smiles.

"Thank you so much, Mr. Winter and please tell Mrs. Winter how much I appreciate it. Your wonderful wife makes the best chowder on the whole island. What a treat this is."

"Will do, Ms. Sandy. Have a good afternoon." He tips his hat to her. "I best be going, as Mrs. Winter will be looking out the window for me wondering where I have gone for so long. She loves to keep tabs on me." He laughs a hearty deep laugh as his eyes scan around the outside of the cottage looking for Margaret. Sandy can see the disappointment on his wrinkled face, as she is nowhere to be found.

He continues, "The weather looks to be stormy later on, so enjoy the sunshine while you can." He nods his head and turns to take his leave. But before he closes his car door he yells, "Please tell Margaret that I said I hope she has a good day too. Oh, I almost forgot, when will Andy be home?"

Sandy stands and yells to him, "In a few days, come 'round to see him, he would love that."

"Will do, Ms. Sandy. Take care now, ya hear."

As Sandy is talking to Mr. Winter, Margaret begins her duties in the kitchen pulling the chicken salad she had made the day before from the fridge.

Sandy hears Stephen fussing back in his bedroom then, so she goes through the deck screen door into the cottage telling Margaret as she passes her in the kitchen that she is going to fetch Stephen from his crib.

"That child has been asleep all morning. He should be in a great mood." Sandy says as she walks down the hall.

"He's always in a good mood, what do you mean?" Margaret laughs.

Sandy appears back in the kitchen in a few moments with a rested Stephen.

"Are you ready for some lunch, sweetie?" Margaret asks Sandy as she enters the kitchen with Stephen.

"Why sure. I love your chicken salad."

"Sandy, my goodness, ever since I met you, your nose hasn't work right. I am sure it is because you are pregnant. Stephen has a dirty diaper on." She reaches for Stephen.

"Whew…little boy, what in the world have you been eating? Slugs from the garden, again?" Margaret asks Stephen as she takes him from Sandy.

The women laugh remembering that day well.

"Thank you, Margaret. And I am famished."

They laugh together again because Sandy is always hungry, even if a bad smell invades the room.

"How are you feeling today, beautiful?" Margaret asks Sandy, as she is finishing up the diaper change. Sandy doesn't have space to answer because Margaret continues on. "I heard Mr. Winter say it is going to storm. I don't believe it. It is such a beautiful day, isn't it? I really don't think that Mr. Winter is right this time. There are barely any clouds in the sky and the ocean is so calm today."

Sandy marvels at how well she and Margaret get along. They work together like clockwork knowing what the other is going to do or say next. And Sandy loves how Margaret asks her several questions all at once and in a row and never leaves her time to answer the first one before she makes a completely unrelated statement.

Sandy grabs the lemonade from the counter and the glasses from the strainer and heads out onto the porch. The wind had picked up some and the wind chime was singing its tune.

Margaret joins Sandy on the deck riding Stephen on her shoulders and ducking him under the doorframe as the two come out the screen door. They are both laughing as they play. Sandy isn't comfortable with having Stephen on the unfinished deck since the railing isn't up yet. "Hey, I am going to grab the play pen. Be right back." Sandy says to her.

Margaret hands Stephen over to Sandy and insists on getting the play pen saying, "Sit here, you should not be lifting heavy things in your condition, how many times have I told you that. You have got to take care of yourself. We don't want anything to happen to that sweet baby in there." With that she pats Sandy's belly, and turns to go get the portable pack-n-play.

Sandy holds her son close, not daring to let him toddle around. Margaret returns quickly with the pack-n-play and an armful of toys. "Stephen will be happy to play in here while we eat our lunch." she says.

After setting up the playpen on the far side of the deck, the two friends sit down at the picnic table to enjoy their lunch. Chatting about nothing and everything, the women enjoy each other's company, as usual.

The sky begins to cloud and the sea begins to froth as the wind picks up in intensity. Looking to the sky, both women realize that Mr. Winter had been right. A terrible storm was coming.

CHAPTER 27

Reflecting

His day had been long; he was tired, and glad to finally be heading home. He had been away from his beloved family for four long months. Andrew was on his last leg of the long journey from Hamburg to London to New York City and ultimately to Portland, Maine.

He missed Sandy and was so anxious to return to her and "Little Bit". He loved calling Stephen "Little Bit" 'cause that is what he was…a little bit of heaven sent to he and Sandy from above. Sandy laughed in a special sweet, motherly way every time she heard him call Stephen by his pet name. He loved her unique laugh and never tired of it. He probably would have quit with the nickname long ago, but the sound of that particular laugh was one of his favorites, so he continued.

Totally relaxed in the jumbo jet flying in first class towards his beloved Maine, Andrew leans his head back on the headrest, asks for a blanket from the attendant, and closes his heavy eyelids. Not able to sleep, he begins to reminisce about his life.

His heart is full now and he thinks how thankful that he is to finally be happy… really, really happy. He remembers that day when he realized how happy he truly was. And that was the day he finally wept. That day, three years ago, was in the Owl's Nest Lighthouse with Sandy after her fall. He wept for Thad and for Jim, his broken marriage to Beth, for his music and then finally for himself. When the tears came, his heart slowly started to mend. Sandy helped him put the broken pieces carefully back together and the emptiness there began to fill with love and happiness.

Andrew looks out the plane window into the night sky thinking of Jim, still his best friend to this day. He still missed 'the long haired, hippie-type' Jim more than he thought he ever would, wanting and needing to talk with him often over the years. He knew Jim would be proud of who he had become since college and he wishes that Jim could see him now as a famous composer, player and most importantly, a good husband and father. But his biggest regret, still to this day, was that he couldn't apologize to his friend for falling in love with Sandy, *his* wife.

He was sure that if Jim hadn't died on that slippery, wet toll way that fateful day, Andrew would not have Sandy now. And in some ways he felt slightly responsible for Jim's death, almost like it had been his wish.

He knew without a shadow of a doubt that Sandy would have never left her husband, and he would have never let her. He saw it as a trade of sorts where he had to give up his best friend to have Sandy-such a cruel, heart-wrenching and ironic twist of fate for all three of them. His best friend's life had ended so that he could have Sandy. Andrew is still sad, even now.

And then his thoughts shift to Beth. He rarely thought of her anymore. Beth, the woman who had held such a spell over him for so long was the "Beauty and the Beast" wrapped up in a stunning package. Beth had been such an aggravating menace in his mind, taunting him and never letting him go…sadly keeping his heart entangled with hers for what seemed like forever.

Even when she became somewhat crazy over the loss of Thad, he still couldn't let her go. A small part of him blamed himself for her craziness.

But thankfully, time has a way of healing the broken hearted. He finally mended and became strong because of Sandy. Beth no longer ruled his heart, even a small part of it. He smiled as he thought of that analogy for Beth…Beauty and the Beast…thank God the beauty was gone in his mind, only the beast remained.

He wondered, as he sat looking out the window, what had happened to her. A friend from Nashville told him several years ago that she still lived there in Nashville with several adopted children. She had never remarried.

If someone had asked him just five years ago if he would remarry again after Beth, he would have never believed that it would be possible for him to love again, let alone marry. Whether it was fate or God or just "their time", it was a momentous day when he laid his tired eyes on Sandy with her turned up freckled nose and her perky toothy smile as she stood on the banks of the wild Maine shore. That was the day that started the beautiful pirouette in his life, turning it around, allowing love to work its way into his heart. He smiled knowing that Sandy was his life and "Little Bit" was a special addition that made his life complete.

Looking back at the tapestry of his life Andrew marveled at its unfolding. His life was simply a miracle. He was grateful that he had been given a second chance at love, and actually, life itself. The delicate repairs to his broken heart were staying firm.

Landing in Portland, Andrew decides not to call Sandy to tell her he is near, but to surprise her. It was after midnight, the ferry had long since stopped running. He would get a motel room near the ferry landing and get on the first boat over to Owl's Nest in the morning. Sandy loved surprises and he loved giving them to her. He knew he could be home to the cottage by tomorrow afternoon, and they could watch the setting sun on the back porch of the cottage together.

CHAPTER 28

Another Ferry, Another Islander

Standing on the top deck of the ferryboat as it approaches the small island of Owl's Nest, Beth is thankful that she had worn her lined raincoat and a scarf this morning. The weather was chilly and breezy and the sea mist and rain continually sprayed her face and hands as she looks towards the approaching shoreline. The rain smells of newness and hope, an elixir for her fractured heart.

Looking to the future, she contemplates the circumstances and turn of events that have brought her here today. Here, where Andrew lives with Sandy, his wife of three years.

Thinking briefly of the man she once loved, she wonders if time has been good to him. Beth thinks of the last time she saw him.

She remembers sitting on the couch with her first adopted baby, Jing Mae, in her arms trying to listen to him as he talked. The sound of his voice always had relaxed and comforted her in the past. But on that day, the words that spilled out of his mouth were contorted, as if the letters were mixed up within them. She tried desperately to focus. Like a bad speaker at a cheap drive in restaurant, she could hear words, but they were unintelligible to her. She was confused and scared. She wanted to reach out to him, but she wasn't able to; her mind would not allow it.

Then the wrestling with her mind began again as she fought to hold on to him. She was tired, so extremely tired of the noise in her head. It got so loud sometimes that it overshadowed everything.

She remembered that day well as she slid into a vast crevasse, unable to pull herself out. It was a very dark day. His voice trailed behind her like music fading into the background as she fell. His voice was coming from a place and time; a time lost to too much pain and heartache.

Finally she succumbed to the power of her mind's voice and allowed herself to hide in the place of dark comfort. It was safe. It was warm. It became her life. And Andrew did not fit into that life.

Immediately turning inward, she catches her reflection in the salt covered window behind her and smiles quickly forgetting Andrew. Reflected in the window is not the feisty abandoned daughter of a crazy mother or the forgotten teenager of her past, but a beautiful woman that *makes* time wait for her.

In contrast to the other elements of fate, time had been kind to her. Proud of the life she has carved out for herself amongst the rubble that was given her so long ago, she becomes even more confident of her reason for travelling to Owl's Nest, Maine; Andrew's home.

CHAPTER 29

The Pact

As in the past, Beth finds herself in a new place and a new situation. Not quite knowing what to expect from Owl's Nest, Maine, this remote and simple part of the world, she feels a little anxious, but is still resolute in her decision.

As the ferryboat cuts across the water, clipping through the fierce and frothy waves, Beth can feel her mind and body get stronger, as she grabs strength from the ocean itself. With the passing of each nautical mile, she becomes even more steadfast. Her objective is clear, just as it has been with every choice she has made in her life.

Approaching the shore, Beth gathers her suitcases that sit around her feet on the deck, and follows the other walk-on passengers to the gangway. She scans the shore road to find a cab. To her disappointment, there are none.

She disembarks and makes her way to the stone stairs that take her up from the dock to the road. She looks to the left and right. Her suitcases are extremely heavy so she places them on the sidewalk and pulls her map from her purse. The map is torn and wrinkled from being viewed so many times in the previous weeks as Beth planned her trip.

She examines it once again to find the red-circled road that would indicate her destination. "Captain's Watch," she reads aloud. Having located her route, she jams the map back into her purse and picks up the suitcases. Since no cabs seem to be available, she comes up with a new plan.

Studying an elderly gentleman across the road from her, she sizes him up. He looks to be in his 80s. He wears overalls and a plaid flannel shirt. He has a beaten up ole fisherman's hat on his head covering his white tuft of hair. A chewed pipe sits in his mouth but no smoke encircles his head. He relaxes on a comfortable wooden bench under a streetlight as he watches the passengers file off the boat.

Beth puts her plan into action. She leaves her bags on the side of the road and runs across the street towards him in her high heels. Putting on her sweetest southern drawl she asks, "Pardon me, Sir. Can you point me in the direction of Captain's Watch? It seems I have lost my way. I am looking for the Madison's Guest House."

Knowing that she is quite beautiful, she takes full advantage of that fact and begins to play the role of the "helpless female', one she plays very well as she stands before the old fisherman looking innocent and vulnerable.

At first the "Mainer" is not impressed with her, as he doesn't like vacationers and worse yet, southerners, on his island. And she is definitely a visitor *and* a southerner. He slowly sizes her up, taking his time. After all, that is all he has.

Eventually he, like every other man before him, falls for her 'female in distress act', and asks her in his politest voice, "Do you have a car, young lady? The Madison's Guest House is up the road quite a distance, too far for a beautiful lady like you to walk."

"No, no I don't." Beth answers as she smiles helplessly up at him.

"All those your bags?" He asks as he points across the road at her pile of suitcases sitting alone across the street.

"Yes, they are," Beth says as she uncontrollably grits her teeth, "I plan on being here awhile."

"Alright then, I guess I can help you. I do live down that way, and I was walking home soon anyways. We will have to walk, I left my car at home today, but I will carry the big one for you. The Madisons are good people."

As he acquiesces to her request, he scuffles across the road to gather her biggest suitcase, suddenly quite happy to be helping this beautiful stranger. Beth thanks the man, delighted that her plan had worked. She walks with him down the road not letting on that she knows exactly where they were going.

They continue down Main Street skirting along the coast for what seems to be half a mile or so and then the old man turns left down Captain's Watch. She knows it is the street because there is an old broken sign that says so nailed to a large tree and pointing in the direction he is turning.

They turn onto a small one-lane dirt road. Not a street at all. There are large pines lining both sides reaching up and touching in the middle above the road. The trees are so dense that they block the sunlight causing it to be gray and dreary. Beth's mood darkens as they turn and proceed down the lane.

The two continue walking for a quite a while and then the man asks, "So, what business you got here in Owl's Nest?"

Upon hearing that innocent and totally appropriate question, Beth stops dead in her tracks, turns slowly towards the stranger and says in a defiant tone and with a glaring evil look, " I don't believe it is *any* of YOUR business what MY business is here. You may take your leave now. I know I can find the Madison's Guest House from here!"

With her dark and cold eyes penetrating deep into his and with her sharp nails cutting into his calloused skin, she grabs her bag from him. The old man stops and releases the handle of her suitcase. Being quite dumbfounded by the stranger's sudden change in attitude and demeanor he wonders what happened that changed her mood. Not knowing, and realizing that he would never guess, he shrugs his shoulders, tips his hat to her and tells her to have a nice day. The old man turns back in the opposite direction leaving her suitcase in the middle of the road.

Realizing that this is not the way to start her stay on the island, Beth yells back an apology to the man. She is not sure that he is able to hear her, as he does not acknowledge her words.

Shrugging her shoulders, she grabs her biggest bag from where it was dropped, and with out another word, she turns away from him and continues down the road. Beth is tired and depressed. Now she is left carrying all her bags, which was *not* her plan at all. The plastic suitcase handle begins to wear blisters on her hands as she makes her way down the road.

Determined, she continues onward as the road is cast with shadows of dusk. She is hoping that the guesthouse is not much further. She had made the decision to leave her car on the mainland to minimize her expenses. Now she wonders if that was a good idea.

Mrs. Madison had told her on the phone several weeks before that her Guest House was the closest one to the ferry landing. Beth counted on it being a bit closer. Rounding the bend in the road, Beth sees an imposing house up ahead. The lights are shining brightly through the windowpanes and as she gets to the clearing surrounding the house, the sun is setting and she knows the night would be upon her in the next hour.

The painted wooden sign in front of the large house reads "Captain Madison's Guest House" in bold letters. She looks up at the house that sits on a little rise before her. A mansion in most areas of the country, it is shingled on the outside with a widow's walk on the roof. It is adorned with many windows and those on the top floor are shuttered, but light shines brightly through all the others.

Taking a deep breath, Beth approaches the wooden staircase going up to the front doors. She runs her fingers through her hair, pinches her cheeks, although she is sure that isn't necessary after the long walk she just endured. She raps on the massive door, and soon a little lady wiping her hands on her apron opens it.

"Hello, dear, nice to see you. I was beginning to worry that you didn't make the last ferry of the day. I am glad you did. Come in, come in."

The older woman pats Beth on the shoulder and grabs her small bag from her hand. Looking behind Beth, she scans the roadway. Not seeing a car, Mrs. Madison asks, "My goodness child, how did you get all these bags all the way up our road from the ferry?

"Oh, it was no problem." Beth lies. Beth glances around the welcoming foyer. It is warm and the glow of a fire in the other room beckons her. A wonderful sweet smell drifts in from the kitchen and Beth's stomach begins to rumble.

"It sure does smell heavenly in here." Beth smiles hoping that is dinner she smells.

"That is dinner cooking, dear. Are you hungry?"

"Now that you ask, I'm starving." Beth answers.

"Let's get you upstairs to your room where you can freshen up before dinner. I am sure you are weary from your trip to our remote little island."

With that Mrs. Madison turns and heads to the center staircase. It is massive with a long stained glass window at the landing where the stairs divide to the left and right. Dark wood banisters and paneled walls make the home warm and inviting even though it is very large.

Beth follows her up the stairs to the right. The stairs curve around where they find the second floor. Mrs. Madison continues up to the third floor where another landing and large window greet them.

"Your suite is up on the third floor. I hope it will be suitable for you. You said you need a quiet get away and this should work perfectly for you." Mrs. Madison says with assurance in her voice.

The ladies make their way down the wooden hallway to the end where there is a large wooden door with a schooner carved delicately into it. Upon the top is a brass plate that simply reads: 8. Mrs. Madison pulls a key from her apron pocket and unlocks the door. She opens it and stands back so that Beth can go in first.

Beth walks into the room and immediately feels welcomed. It is grand and smells of wood and sea salt. There are three large floor-to-ceiling windows across the back wall, where heavy forest green velvet drapes frame each one. A heavily carved antique canopied bed is to her left. The walls are paneled and painted a sea green. There is a Queen Anne's chair and small table next to the bed. The bedspread and canopy are made from gold brocade that flows down the sides in folds of fabric. The ceiling is high and a beautiful crystal chandelier hangs above her head. Beth is very impressed with the room. She decides she made the right choice by staying in this particular guesthouse.

Mrs. Madison begins to explain that this room, The Sea Foam Room, was Captain Madison's wife's bedroom. The windows face the sea so she could watch for her husband's ship to return home.

"Unfortunately for her, he met his demise at sea," she explains, "and left his widow, the original Mrs. Madison, alone and heartbroken. This is the grandest room in the house, my dear."

Mrs. Madison continues to tell of the Captain, who is a distant relative of her husband's, and that her husband inherited this fine house from his grandparents sixty years ago. She opens the simple door to the right side of the room, and motions for Beth to follow. "This is the Captain's bedroom." She continues. "He had direct access to his wife's room, of course, but I think this room will do nicely for what you told me that your needs are."

Through the door is a comfortable sitting area complete with a couch, two overstuffed chairs angled perfectly towards the row of windows allowing the occupants the best view of the sea. On the other side is a small bed and chest of drawers. The walls are painted a darker shade of green than the widow's room. Antlers and busts of every animal imagined decorate the walls. The large fireplace is glowing with a newly laid fire.

"Here is the bathroom, dear." Mrs. Madison points out. "I hope this suite will be to your liking. I must tend to dinner. It will be served at exactly six o'clock. We have no other guests coming tonight so you will join me and my husband in the dining room then."

"Thank you, Mrs. Madison. It smells wonderful and I look forward to dining with you." Beth says as Mrs. Madison leaves the room. With the warmth of the fire's glow and the low light of the lamps, Beth's mood lightens. She scans the space and smiles knowing that this suite will be perfect.

Taking in all the masculine details of the Captain's room, she notices a frame on the wall by the window. It is small and doesn't fill the space well or fit the décor of the beautifully detailed room. Walking over to investigate, she decides it must be something of significance or it would not be hanging in such a magnificent room.

Beth sees a faded ancient scroll inside the frame; its edges worn and paper yellowed. Hardly able to make out the beautifully inscribed words, Beth takes the frame off the nail and carries it over to the lamp where she can read it better. She reads the poem.

The Accounting

Oh, you foolish sailors and captains of the fleet.
You ignore my power with your petty greed and your human deceit.
You take my treasures with no thought of the cost,
And whatever accounting you have taken, you have purposefully lost.

There will come a time, when the books are balanced
For I too take account of your worthless coins and your worthless talents.
Mine is a powerful and majestic reckoning role,
Which can only balance the books with the *taking* of a soul.

Author Unknown

Beth pauses, specifically unnerved by the words, "taking of a soul" written at the end of the poem. She understands what tremendous power those words would have to a sea captain. Pondering the meaning there as she takes the frame back to the wall, she feels something loose on the back of the frame.

Turning the antique frame over, she finds a folded piece of paper stuck between the frame and the back. Beth gently pulls at the paper as to not rip it and walks back over to the lamp. Opening up the paper she sees that it is a hand-written note. The handwriting is exquisite, reminiscent of the penmanship from years gone by. The paper is crumbled and stained but Beth can easily make out the handsomely emblazoned words.

My Dearest Love,

I must leave you once again as I sail the seas. My heart aches for I will miss you. Please pray that the angry lady of the sea won't collect her payment today, as my crew and I head into her unforgiving waters. Your daily prayers and faith remain steadfast and are immensely important to me.

I am forever yours,

Your loving Captain

Beth's eyes begin to water as she replaces the lovely note back where she had found it, and carefully hangs the frame on the wall. Saddened by what she now understands must have been the actions of the grieving widow. The Captain's wife must have fastened the heartfelt last words of her departed husband to the back of the poem, realizing her prayers of safety for her husband went unanswered as the sea claimed his soul on his last voyage. Her Captain's most feared nightmare had come true.

Suddenly distraught by the history of this old house, Beth walks to the windows to see her view of the 'lady of the sea'. She sees that she is lovely. She is strong and unforgiving, wild, and untamed. Beth resonates with her, understanding her fury.

Stunned by the scene through the wavy glass of the ancient window of the Captain's bedroom, Beth imagines his widow standing where she stands, many years before, looking out to the sea bearing an ache in her heart, as she longs for her sea-faring husband.

Beth witnesses the transformation of the sea's color due to the setting of the sun. It is as if a skilled artist adds another layer of pigment on top of the brilliant blue that is underneath, changing it to a deeper tint of that same color. Slowly, the hue changes to a darker steel-like color mimicking a gigantic steel door that is shut and locked. Beth's mood deviates again to her dour, inner self as an ever-present blackness fills her. Standing at the window she marvels at the ocean's primal nature-one that could not nor would not be tamed.

Being captivated by an inanimate object is rare for Beth, and she soon realizes that she is enthralled by its spell over her. She becomes mesmerized by its allure. The voice of the sea resonates with the beat of her own heart telling her that she will soon have the peace she craves. But this peace that she seeks will come at a cost.

Having no fear of the sea's enticement, Beth opens her heart and the latch that holds the wind and sea at bay, welcoming its fury. Her black tendrils of hair whip around her face as the wind and sea spray sting her skin as if tentacles of a violent sea creature. She embraces the sea and welcomes its power, suddenly feeling confident in her convictions.

The raw cold and sudden rush of air overtakes her slight frame, forcing her back into the room. Holding steadfast to the window frame, Beth stands secure in her resolve. She smiles. Her smile is one of acknowledgement, knowing that she will not surrender to the tempting seduction of the sea, like the sailors of the past who succumbed to the ocean's beauty and power. Nor is she willing to take the role of the captain's wife, standing by as the ocean takes her captain, for payment. Instead, Beth comes to an accord with the sea, conceding to its demand for a soul.

Fully exposed, but never vulnerable, she makes her vow to the sea. She nods and accepts its challenge, as she cries out to the wildness before her, "You will have your soul, but it won't be mine."

Feeling omnipotent and more certain of her mission than ever she closes the window and turns her back to the sea, ignoring her cries.

With her vow to the sea being as fresh in her mind as the air in her room, she slowly stokes the fire and then retraces her steps to the widow's bedroom and places her suitcases on the bed. There is a tall chest of drawers on one wall, so she spends the majority of the next hour organizing her clothes. When finished, she stows her suitcases in the large wardrobe by the door.

Changing her clothes, Beth chooses a simple dress and white sweater to put on for dinner.

CHAPTER 30

Returning Home

Andrew arrives on Owl's Nest the next morning.

As Andrew leaves the ferry dock on Main Street, his heart starts racing. He loves the fact that after three years of marriage, his heart still beats in eager anticipation of when he is going to see Sandy again. While he adored playing his music for appreciative fans, four months was too long to be away from those that held his heart. He was delighted that he was almost home in the arms of his beautiful wife and small son.

Following through on his plan to surprise Sandy, he rented a car in Portland and drove for four hours to arrive at the dock to board the ferry to come home. Once on the island he returned the rental to a small car return business run by Manny Whitman.

Andrew had known Manny almost as long as he had owned his cottage. Manny was a competent businessman and a great guy. Andrew had used his services many times since starting his new career. It was a long way to Portland, and he rarely wanted Sandy and Stephen to make the journey there to pick him up from, or deliver him to the airport.

When he arrives at the rental lot, Manny offers to give him a ride home, but he refuses, saying that a walk on this beautiful late summer afternoon would do him good. Manny would be closing soon, so he asks if he can store his luggage at the shop until tomorrow.

"Of course you can…no problem, Andy." Manny replies. With that, Manny helps Andrew pull presents for Stephen from one of his bags, placing them into his backpack.

"Thanks Manny. I'll be seeing you tomorrow."

"Sure thing, Andy."

Manny locks up his shop as Andrew begins his short walk. The walk from Manny's is exhilarating. It is a short walk, and he thinks of Sandy with her newly cropped hair, slight body, and wide smile. He is excited to see her, to hold her, and to love her.

There is a slight brisk breeze in the late afternoon air that invigorates Andrew even more. The spruces are bending slightly as their tops give off a fresh pine scent that always reminds him of home. How lucky he is to live on this tiny island where the rest of the crazy world is far, far away.

Walking down the road lined on both sides with cottages of his neighbors Andrew stops at Charlie's cottage gate to ask him for a pink rose as he sees him tending his garden.

"Hell, yeah, take a dozen." Charlie says to him.

"Thanks so much, Charlie, but one will do."

"Will I see you next week at the bar? I think Joe is playing his harmonica or some such nonsense," Charlie says as he returns to his gardening.

The two laugh, as they both know that Joe plays a terrible harmonica. "Maybe, if Sandy will let me leave the house," Andrew laughs knowing that he would not want to leave either.

"Okay, Andy…see you around. Are you home for a while now?" he asks.

"Yep. I am. Gotta run, I'm going to surprise Sandy. She doesn't know I am in town yet."

"Get on then. Good to have you back."

CHAPTER 31

The Ocean

Stephen sits in the pack-n-play sorting his toys into piles. The two friends laugh at his organizational skills.

"Hey, after lunch, will you go up to the barn for me and pull out an old sign that is sitting near the barn doors?" Sandy asks Margaret. I want to set it out to stick by the front door when Andrew returns tomorrow. He will get a kick out of it."

Margaret answers her, "Sure, be happy to." But Margaret seems distracted and deep in thought. The wind chimes start to sing once again, but this time with more intensity and volume.

"The ocean is getting wild, with the wind picking up." Margaret finally says as she looks out to the sea.

"Yeah, it is. Mr. Winter sure does know these waters, doesn't he?" Sandy answers.

Margaret doesn't answer her, but gets up off the bench where they are sitting next to each other and goes to stand on the other side of the deck, looking towards the ocean and the rocks below.

"Sandy, you love the ocean, don't you?" she says.

"Well, if the truth be known, no, I do not really like it. It scares me sometimes. *And...*you need to back up from the edge of the deck; *you* are making me nervous!" Sandy tells Margaret.

"Why," Margaret wants to know.

"Because it is dangerous, and I don't want to have to find another Nanny." Sandy laughs.

"Why don't you like the ocean, Sandy?"

"It's not that I don't like it. I think it is absolutely beautiful. But I prefer to look at it from a distance. We have had a rough past, water and me." Sandy giggles.

Trying to end the conversation about the ocean Sandy says, "You have never seen me down on the shore much, have you?"

"Come to think about it, I haven't.

Glad that Sandy had averted that subject she went on to tell Margaret how delicious her chicken salad is. "Is this a new recipe?" She asks.

"Yes, it has grapes in it. I am glad you like it," Margaret tells her as she looks to Stephen who has fallen asleep.

Margaret leaves the edge of the deck and the ocean to assume her nanny duties. She walks over to the pack-n-play, and carefully lifts Stephen up and whispers to Sandy, "I'll be back, I am going to put him in his crib."

"Okay, but hurry back, you haven't touched your chicken salad. And thanks." Sandy sits there enjoying the breeze and the fact that she had such a great nanny.

CHAPTER 32

The Confrontation

Beth walks into the small café on the far side of Owl's Nest. It felt good to take a brisk walk to the café this afternoon in the sunshine. For fear of running into Andrew, she hadn't gone out much since coming to the island. Besides the tour of the island she had on her second day, and her walk to the boutique hairdresser's studio this morning, she had remained at the guesthouse. Just this morning she had decided to cut her long hair, above her shoulders, since it was summer and she was in a good mood.

She was glad that Melody had called her. Wanting to keep a low profile, she wears her 'Nashville Sounds' baseball cap, large oversized jacket and sunglasses.

She is anxious and a little nervous for her luncheon date with her old friend, Melody. She had been somewhat surprised that her friend was also on the island on holiday. It had been years since she had seen or heard from her. The call had caught her off guard, and she was skeptical of why Melody just happened to be on this particular island at this particular time. Beth had gone through many changes since her days on the street, but she had never lost her sense for danger.

As Beth enters the restaurant, she scans the small diner. Melody sits at a small table at the far end of the room with her back to the window. She is sipping her usual drink of choice, chardonnay. Her childhood friend hadn't changed much over the years; still the beauty that she always was.

Beth walks up to the table quickly, sits down facing Melody as to not draw any attention to herself and smiles at her friend. The two reach out across the table to grab each other's hands. It is good to see her again. The waiter comes up momentarily to hand Beth the menu and ask her what she would be drinking this afternoon. Without looking at the waiter, she answers, "I would love a glass of chardonnay, like my friend here."

The waiter hesitates only for a moment, and then smiles and responds, "Yes Madam, right away." He turns to tend to her request.

The two women begin their visit with all the normal things that old friends talk about when they haven't seen each other in a while. Melody tells her of her kids and husband, and how she is getting fatter and fatter the older she gets. They laugh together as Beth tells her that she is still beautiful.

Melody mentions then that she is thinking about having a few "tucks" here and there and Beth snickers as she talks of the procedures. Beth tells her once again that she doesn't think she needs any work done because she is perfect just the way she is.

Beth talks lovingly of her children for a few minutes telling Melody what sports and lessons they were doing. Then she complains that they are growing up too fast, and that they didn't seem to need her as much anymore. They all had become so independent.

Melody reminds her, with her sensible words, "That is what you want for your children, Beth. You want them to become more and more independent because one day, they must leave the nest." Beth dismisses Melody's opinion on the matter just like she had done many times before.

Changing the subject, Melody asks, "So, you have cut your hair, I see. That surprises me, why did you do that?"

Beth begins to get uncomfortable and she squirms in her seat. She wishes that Melody would talk of pleasant things and not bring up things that upset her. It seemed to her that Melody *always* brings up those things that upset her.

Melody, noting her reluctance to answer adds, "Well, then what brings you to Owl's Nest, Beth?"

Rather curtly, Beth remarks, "I cut my hair because I wanted to; I needed a change, that's all there is to it. I just wanted to.

Thinking for a moment, with her impatience starting to get the best of her, Beth continues, "And Melody, I will tell you *why* I came here." Her voice waivers slightly as she continues, "You are my oldest friend, and it seems I can never skirt the truth with you, can I?" She laughs ingenuously, and continues.

"I am not needed as much by my children anymore as I have told you many times before. They are growing up. I want a baby again. I am here to get one."

Melody looks at her friend with disdain and contempt as the waiter brings Beth her wine. When the waiter leaves, Melody asks pointedly, "What? You already have four children, how many is the magic number, Beth?"

"It is different this time." Beth tells her. "You wouldn't understand." She takes a slow sip of her chardonnay dismissing her friend.

"*What* child, Beth? You know you can't do what you are thinking. You can't just decide that you need a baby, Beth."

Defiantly, Beth answers her rather loudly. "I am getting a baby here and you can't stop me Melody." Beth looks around the café to see that some folks at nearby tables are staring at her. But she continues her rant, "This is not the place to discuss this, Melody. I will talk to you later about this."

"No! We will talk about this now." Melody answers, matching Beth's intensity with her own defiance and anger.

Knocking over her glass of wine as she stands, Beth screams at Melody, "You don't get to decide *when* I talk about *what*, Melody. I am a grown woman. We can talk about this later, in *private*."

Knowing how Beth rationalizes things, Melody insists. "I am not going to leave this island until you explain what you are going to do, Beth."

At this point, Beth is glaring at Melody across the table. She smacks her hands on the table with a loud slapping noise, as she bends forward to look closely into her best friend's eyes. Beth's face becomes red and distorted as her anger boils within. Her voice gets louder and louder with each word spoken.

"Well, *perfect* Melody, you can rot on this island for all I care, cause I will NEVER tell you what I am up to. What I do here is none of your business. You are nothing but a busybody anyways. You keep getting into my business, always trying to tell me what I should or shouldn't do. I won't listen to your reasoning anyway. In fact, I will never listen to you again. You disgust me!" At this point Beth is totally out of control and everyone in the café becomes silent.

Upon hearing Beth's loud voice echoing across the room, the owner of the establishment, Ben Johnson, runs over to Beth's table as quickly as he can with the waiter in tow. He begins to sop up the spilled wine and asks her to please be quiet. He gently takes her arm, lifts her chair back into place, and helps her sit back down.

The diners, frozen in their seats, have stopped eating, and are staring in Beth's direction wondering why this woman is screaming in the café like she is.

Once Mr. Johnson gets her seated again, he pleads with her, "Please calm down miss; is something wrong?" The minute those words come from his mouth he knows he shouldn't have asked her that question.

"Yes, there is something wrong!" Beth screams at the man. "I will not be staying in this cafe and I am not ordering any food, cause I am leaving! I don't like the company here." Grabbing her purse from the floor, she glares at Melody one last time, and then gets up, glaring too at Mr. Johnson, as if it is his fault. Beth rushes out of the café bumping into several of the diners as she leaves.

The waiter and Mr. Johnson whisper together quietly over at Beth's table as they quickly pick up the knocked over wine glass and wipe it clean. Then Mr. Johnson turns and apologizes for the commotion as he pushes in Beth's chair.

The waiter grabs the menu from Beth's place and goes to the door to seat the next waiting party at the table, hoping the other diners will soon forget the commotion. An elderly woman is next in line.

"Please follow me Ma'am, I have a table for one over here in the corner. He pulls out the single chair at the table where Beth was sitting just moments before.

As the waiter leaves the menu with her, and apologizes once again for the commotion, the woman now seated there turns to the couple sitting next to her and asks, "What in the world just happened at this table? It seems that woman was quite upset."

"Oh, yes. She was screaming like she was in an argument with someone seated across from her. She was saying something about a child that she wanted and a woman rotting on the island." She is crazy, that is all. We were just trying to figure out who she is." All the other diners go back to eating their lunches discussing the events that just happened, glad summer season with all the crazy tourists would be over in a few months.

Once outside, Beth begins to calm down wishing that the whole argument hadn't happened. She hadn't wanted to draw attention to herself, but she was tired of Melody and her voice of reason. Melody never listened to her and never agreed with her anymore. And Beth was tired of that. Perhaps she needed to find a new best friend. As far as Beth was concerned, she never wanted to see Melody again. And more than anything, she didn't want Melody to mess up her carefully planned trip here to Owl's Nest. She was here for one reason and she wasn't going to be talked out of this one.

Beth strides away quickly from the café, pulling her cap down lower, in hopes that no one there recognized her as the woman staying at The Madison's Guest House. Almost back to the guesthouse, she begins to put a shorter time frame on her plan, so she can start to put it into practice immediately. The less time she is on this dreadful island, the better, she decides.

CHAPTER 33

Homecoming

As Andrew sees his cottage from down the road, he once again marvels at its simple structure and homey feeling. He can afford a much grander house now, but he and Sandy both love the cottage. It is home; a typical Maine cottage to some, but so much more to both of them.

He and Sandy had done some fantastic improvements to the place over the last three years. The best by far was the addition of a gourmet kitchen to the far left side. Sandy loves to cook, and the small wall of a kitchen that he had before they married simply wasn't large enough. When they expanded the cottage, they also vaulted the roof making the small space seem much larger. His discovery of ten heavy antique beams at a salvage place last year was incorporated into the structure of the cottage as rafters, making it more rustic and "Maine" like. He was pleased with the results.

He also had built a large wooden deck to the side of the kitchen. It overlooks the vast ocean and rocks below. The view from there is outstanding. He knows he will spend many meals sitting on that deck with Sandy and 'Little Bit', overlooking his beloved sea while he is home. He plans on finishing it, adding the metal and glass railings to the sides as quickly as possible. It is not safe the way it is for a toddler, or adults for that matter.

Working on the upcoming project in his mind, he continues walking up the dirt road that leads to the cottage. As his mind is doing the math for the rails, he sees the honeymoon sign sitting by the front door. He laughs out loud knowing that Sandy would have thought that would be a funny welcome-home gift. He could hardly wait to grab Sandy and hold her, kiss her, and thank her for that great memory - his *welcome home* gift.

As if his wish instantaneously comes true, he sees her standing on the deck, with her back to him, looking out to the sea. He quickens his step to match the racing of his heart. She stands there wearing a white t-shirt, and bright green shorts, her normal summer attire. He can't wait to hold her tightly in his arms. What a great surprise he had for her. He is home!

As Andrew approaches the newly built porch, he puts his backpack containing Stephen's presents and a change of clothes on the ground, under the deck, and tiptoes the rest of the distance to her. As a fleeting thought, he wonders where Toby is.

Sandy doesn't seem to hear him come up behind her. As he gets closer, he is amazed at her tiny frame and beautiful long legs. Even though she is carrying their second child in her belly, she remains as attractive as ever.

Creeping ever so slowly towards her, Andrew's desires overtake him and he wants nothing more than to run up to her and embrace her wildly, but he controls the urge and remains stealthy. Andrew approaches her with extreme caution as to not startle her because he sees that she is very close to the edge of the deck.

He notices then that she has changed her hair color…it is several shades darker than the bright red that he loves. He is taken back somewhat by the choice she has made. He decides not to say anything to her about it, as it must have been something she wanted to surprise him with.

Wanting to call out her name but hesitating, he quietly takes off his shoes instead. In his sock feet, he steps up the stairs and onto the deck behind her. The waves are smashing loudly against the rocks below with that familiar fierceness that he loves although with an intensity that he doesn't remember. He knows she can't hear him as he approaches.

Reaching for her, he tenderly places his arms gently around her chest feeling her softness; he nibbles on her neck, recognizing the fragrance of his favorite perfume. His kisses cascade down to her shoulders. He begins to turn her slowly around as he closes his eyes and tenderly kisses her lips.

As he does so, a loud gasp comes from his kiss. It almost takes him down. It is a gasp of shock. His breath is gone and he has no air left in his lungs. The passionate kiss that Andrew receives is not Sandy's. He opens his eyes. His disbelief at what he sees is horrifying. He shakes his hands from her waist.

Seeing *her*, his mouth falls open and his eyes became even wider with disbelief.

The woman that used to be his everything, the very woman that used to take his breath away all those years ago, and the one that took him so long to forget, is standing before him on his deck, at his cottage in Owls Nest, Maine! And once again she had taken his breath. But this time, it is out of shock and then alarm.

His mind races, and an important question nags…why did she look and smell so much like Sandy? His words for her won't come. All the words that he had stored away for years won't come.

She smiles up at him then…one that is almost familiar but not quite. Her smile is sinister and disturbing. A smile that Andrew finds frightening. There, before him, so close to him that he can feel the coolness radiating from her skin, *is* Beth! She is Beth in body, but her emerald eyes are vacant, almost unrecognizable. Evil.

Beth…his first love.

Beth…the mother of Thad.

Beth…the woman who broke his heart.

Beth…*the* crazy one.

And Beth…the Beauty and the Beast.

She is here, with him now on Owl's Nest. But how can that be? Is he having a nightmare? Questions jump around in his mind, questions that he needs answers for, but his voice still won't come.

Why are you here?

How did you find me?

And…Where is Sandy and Little Bit?

Then he realizes that those are answers he is afraid to know.

Andrew turns from 'the beast' suddenly and sprints into the cottage through the screen door. Searching frantically, he scurries from room to room. His skin marinates in sweat as he drips with anxiety. Numbness devours his mind and body as the sea continues to serenade him with its vulgar melody.

"Sandy!! Sandy!" he screams at the top of his lungs. He cannot hear her voice as his senses are bombarded with the ferocious sounds and smells of the growling sea. The sound becomes so intense that Andrew finds himself being pulled towards her and her cries. As if a magnetic force, he succumbs to the power and steps out onto the small deck on the back of the cottage. He looks frantically over to Sandy's favorite spot, the porch swing. It is swinging violently, but she is not there. Sea spray slaps him and knocks him to the deck. He looks up to see Toby cowering in the corner of the porch. His head is down and he is shaking. Andrew reaches for Tobe. "What is it boy?" Recognizing his voice, Toby comes slowly over to Andrew with his tail between his legs and sits next to his best friend. Reading Toby's face, Andrew knows the unthinkable has happened.

The tide is high and it begins to devour the steps, tearing them apart with a viciousness that he has never seen before. The sea is angry. The waves froth and foam as if a rabid dog. His heartthrobs penetrate his being and Andrew knows his mind and body is suddenly in total tempo and unison with the wild pulsating Lady of the Sea. Andrew screams out to her, wrestling with the words he must ask. "What has Beth done?"

The sea calms as Andrew listens. Her cries are of deceit and deception. They speak of injustice and loss. And finally she weeps for love, a love so deep that nothing else matters.

Ultimately…Andrew understands. His beloved Maine, a respite from his past, turns on him in that moment, leaving him exposed. He moans in savage agony and in synchronicity with the breathings of the sea.

CHAPTER 34

New Beginnings

B eth, with Stephen in tow, quietly boards the ferry to leave Owl's Nest behind forever, bound for their life together as mother and son. She leaves behind her hennas acts, discarded remnants of a sick mind. Memories that she will soon forget, and a life there on Owl's Nest that she will make sure Stephen won't remember. Her mission almost complete, she smiles sweetly, looking dearly at the little boy beside her.

"I love you, Thaddeus. It has always been you my sweet boy." She sweetly whispers to Stephen. The toddler reaches for her hand and says, "I wuv you too, Margaret."

"Where are we going?" he adds with excitement dancing in his eyes.

"We are going to a place where you will meet your brothers and sisters, and see our new home. You will be happy there, Thaddeus." Beth lovingly tells him.

Stephen smiles up at his nanny.

"Am I going to be a big brother?" he asks. "Do you have a baby in your tummy, like Mommy?

Beth doesn't answer the child. She looks out to the now distant island of Owl's Nest; the one that is rapidly disappearing from her view and her mind.

Beth's mind is almost in total darkness now, something necessary for her to survive. This darkness covers all her actions of late, as if a dark Band-Aid placed upon a horrific act, erasing it from her memory. Before the last flicker of light and saneness departs from her mind, she is forced to revisit the crime she committed there one last time.

CHAPTER 35

Final Payment

Margaret had had a lovely lunch with Sandy that day, the day of Sandy's death. Sandy was relaxing on the deck at the picnic table when she arrived with Mr. Winter. It was a beautiful summer day with beautiful blue skies and an exceptionally calm ocean.

Margaret sat next to Sandy and they talked. They dreamed aloud of Andrew and how he would be home in a few days, and how excited Sandy was to see him again. Sandy talked about how happy she would be when Andrew could finally meet Margaret.

Beth remembers listening with a pleasant smile on her face, but torment mixed with agony as well a deep longing filled her heart and mind. She would see Andrew again that was for sure. However, she knew terror and horror would fill his heart when he did. Her well-laid plan, her mission, was almost complete…this plan that took so many years to organize and accomplish, a plan that had played out perfectly. She could hardly wait for it to take place.

It was easy really. She had laid the last bit of groundwork for the past weeks as she had lived on the island as Margaret Buchannan. She had planted everything in the islander's minds that she needed them to understand and discover.

Beth had carefully fertilized the seeds that she planted. She fed her garden with clues and evidence that she scattered around the cottage and with the people she met. She had planted a garden of ammunition for the police to find. She was an outstanding gardener, always having tended the garden of 'mistaken reality' well.

She was proud of what she had accomplished on Owl's Nest, Maine. Leaving no stones unturned, Andrew would be her scapegoat, the proprietor of her crime.

As if watching a horror movie, Beth plays out the final scene in her mind's eye as Margaret acts out her part to perfection. Real life characters played their parts as expected. The sea itself performed its dance in beautiful harmony with the sky, the rocks, and the wind.

The Emmy award winning performance, with such a grand finale, was more than she had anticipated. It all began when Sandy hired Margaret as her nanny just as she had meticulously planned, four weeks prior. Margaret had quickly gained Sandy's and Stephen's trust. Delores and Sue and even Ernesto stunned her with their performances.

The perfectly scripted finale ended beautifully with a simple question posed to Sandy-a question she already knew the answer to.

After taking Stephen into the cottage for his nap, Margaret returns to the deck to eat her chicken salad. She proceeds with her well-thought out questions to Sandy.

"Sandy, you love the ocean don't you?" Margaret asks.

"Well, if the truth be known, No, I do not really like it. It scares me."

"Why?" Margaret asks.

"Oh it's a long story and I don't like talking about it really." I don't mind looking at it from a distance like this, but I am not fond of being near it. You have never seen me down on the shore much, have you?"

Margaret continues with her scripted dialogue, "They say the sea seduces those that love her, and she longs for their souls."

Sandy, playing her part flawlessly, looks at Margaret for a long moment giving so much emotion to the scene, then laughingly says, "I am glad that I don't love the sea then. Come on, Margaret enough silly talk about the sea. I don't really like it, yet here I am living on the ocean! Kind of ironic isn't it."

"No, I think it is meant to be...*you* and the *sea*." Margaret longingly looks to sea, beckoning it to come forward as she gets up from the bench.

"You see, Sandy, the sea and I have a special bond. I made a vow to the sea many weeks ago from the window of my inn. The sea spoke to me on my first evening here."

Margaret leisurely, but deliberately, walks over to the edge of the deck.

"Oh, Margaret, you are talking like the sea is alive. It is inanimate and cannot speak to anyone. Come on silly, let's stop this ridiculous talk of the sea."

Staying completely in character, Margaret doesn't move from her position next to the edge of the deck as she continues to stare out to the ocean, listening.

As she feels the wind pick up, right on cue, she steadies herself.

"Sandy, come here. Look out there and listen." Margaret points to the sea. "Do you hear the Lady of the sea calling out to you?"

Beth sees Sandy look at Margaret with a nervousness that excites her. Sandy gets up from the bench where she is sitting, and walks over to where Margaret stands.

"No, I don't hear the sea calling to me? Why, is it calling out to you? What does its voice sound like?" Sandy jokes as she takes a step back from the edge of the deck.

Taking her unrehearsed cues from Sandy, Margaret grabs Sandy's arm and puts her other arm around her waist, pulling her close to her body as well as closer to the edge, above the waiting rocks.

Margaret whispers in Sandy's ear, "You must hear the sea; it *is* calling to you. It is seeking a soul...*your* soul."

Margaret kisses Sandy on the cheek then.

Sandy looks to Margaret, with a sudden fear in her eyes, as Margaret's hand tightens on her arm.

"You are hurting me!" Sandy struggles to pull away.

Beth is prepared for Sandy's 'fight and flight' scene. Having thought of every scenario beforehand, she only laughs. Tightening her grip on Sandy's arm, Beth looks into her eyes for a minute longer and then asks with a devilish smile on her face, "Do you know who I am Sandy?

As Beth doesn't wait for her answer, Margaret sings sweetly to Sandy. "Sweet dreams my Sandy, sweet dreams my sweet."

The push is a hard one. Sandy loses her balance and tumbles over the edge. As an added unrehearsed bonus, Beth hears herself yell down to Sandy, overtaking the sound of the waves, "I am Beth!" And she laughs.

All it took was one hard push. With that push, Sandy tumbles onto the rocks below. Her body lay broken and battered. Beth watches Sandy's body for a long time.

The rocks below accept Sandy's body, and then as planned, Sandy is offered to the sea.

In the ebb of the tide, the sea retrieves its gift, grateful for another soul. Beth keeps watching as the sea devours Sandy's limp body. Soon her crimson blood left on the rocks is washed into the sea becoming one with the water.

The final act was a simple one. That one act spanned only a few moments of time, but ended a lifetime of torment for Beth. In one last word to the sea, Beth shouts, "You have your payment, it is Sandy, not me. And I have my treasure!"

She turns on her heel, shunning the sea and opens the screen door as she steps into the cottage.

CHAPTER 36

Transformation

Beth eagerly enters the familiar room within the familiar house to gather her treasure. She enters with a feeling of weightlessness that is alien to her. Her dream of what seemed to span a lifetime is finally coming true.

Her feet seem to float ever so lightly across the wooden floor. This incredible dream-like state she finds herself in is exuberating. Her heart beats with a ferociousness that is addicting. The feeling is good, so good, that she begins to feel a deep contentment within her being telling her that what she had done is right and good and true.

She is intently focused on the crib on the far wall of the small room. The room is dimly lit, but a luminescence seems to glow brightly from above the crib bathing the young child below. Concentrating on her task at hand as she is drawn to the scene before her. The day had threatened rain; it was held back by a force that Beth knew to be her own.

Reaching the other side of the small room, Beth slowly peers inside the crib. The sweet boy sleeps. Love cloaks her heart and her breath is momentarily taken away as she takes him in. He is covered in a cotton blanket. The only part of him that she can see is his perfectly shaped head and ivory face. His lips pucker pink with a slight upturn to them. His eyelids remain closed. She recognizes his ears then and smiles. Though she knows somewhere inside that she didn't give birth to this child, she recognizes once again that he is intended for her.

Beth reaches out her shaking hands towards him. Suddenly she is held back. The feel of his soft skin is replaced with questions…questions that push their way from deep inside and surface in her confused mind. She hates questions that want answers; questions that she doesn't ask; questions that confuse her and questions that ruin her perfect moments. She knows she doesn't have to answer them and she waits for them to fade into the pool of the unanswered.

Melody speaks to her then, "I have been patient with you, Beth. For all these years, I have been patient with you." Beth does not turn towards the voice, still waiting for her confusion to go away. She remains silently focused on her child.

Her 'voice of reason' continues, "I have been your friend and your helper from the time you were a little girl. You cripple me now with your barbaric actions. I so wish you had listened to me over the years. I tried, to no avail, one last time to get through to you in the café. But you wouldn't listen, would you? I am your voice of reason but you have shunned me and gone too far now. It is too late. I can no longer tolerate you and your behavior. Today, with this act of violence, you and I will forever part our ways. You will be left alone in your darkness. Good bye, Beth."

Beth realizes that her only friend is deserting her. But, she is not sad. She has been deserted so many times before, that one more time won't matter. She and Melody had fought and battled throughout most of her life and she too, knew it was time for them to part ways. She waits, gaining more strength. The confusion, the questions and Melody all fade away. They fade into the recesses of her fragile mind. And Melody takes with her the only bit of goodness left inside Beth's heart.

Beth moves time with her mind, and settles on a memory from long ago...a time when life *was* good and her baby boy, Thaddeus, slept ever so peacefully in his crib.

Her smile and reassurance come back as she lovingly gazes down at her child. This boy, her everything, is and will always will be, hers. Beth reaches for her child.

The present becomes the past and Beth is comfortable there. Words come from her mouth that she wasn't expecting although she knew to be true. "Mama is here, my sweet boy, Mama is here." She leaves a room within a house with her son in her arms as her aching heart is healed.

Time is a fragile thing that knows no bounds. It races in and out of a confused and hurting mind changing circumstances and people. And even a heart.

CHAPTER 37

Beth's Garden

With her mission accomplished, Beth's garden would grow at a rapid speed. Only Andrew would be privy to the fact that she, *Beth,* **was** the gardener; the one that had orchestrated the rest of his life, the gardener who would slowly poison him as he rotted away in jail. And…most importantly, she was the gardener that killed his beloved Stephen and Sandy.

Beth thought of her mother, Jackie, whom had thrown her away all those years ago…for a man, her father. Her own mother had thrown her away, like garbage and forgotten her. Then Andrew had thrown her away as well and had forgotten her. But she hadn't forgotten him. She had followed his life, his career, and his whereabouts over the years and hatched a flawless plan, one that came to fruition beautifully.

Fading into the dark recesses of her mind, Owl's Nest, Maine, the speck of land still on the horizon and the people there, would soon completely disappear from her mind.

Beth turns to Thaddeus, "Yes, sweet darling, Thaddeus, I have a baby in my tummy, it's your little sister. She bends down to look him in the eyes. "Will you help me come up with a name for her? I am thinking of, perhaps, Ernesta? What do you think?" Thaddeus shakes his head in agreement.

Beth rubs her abdomen. She feels her own heartbeat there and wonders, but only for a moment, how such an empty heart could have such a steady beat.

She looks to her forearm, her steady reminder of what is most important to her, and reads silently as she had done so many times before. But this time, she pulls her sleeve higher up her arm, past the words that were scripted all those years ago, and reads the new words she recently added.

Always Thaddeus,
Always mine,
'Til the end of time

CHAPTER 38

Hope

Sunlight filters through the trees into the small single window behind his head. The concrete floor shines with a sheen that reflects the light streaming in through the patterned screen. The walls are plastered with photos of Sandy and Stephen and poems he had written, sonnets from his broken heart.

He looks towards the door with its small barred window and sees the single light bulb hanging from the ceiling outside the door. He sits slouching on his bed, leaning up against the cold brick wall, looking into the deserted hall before him.

Andrew waits.

He waits for justice.

He waits on time.

He waits for his broken heart to fall apart and then die altogether.

Sandy and "Little bit" seem like only a memory now.

One he struggles to remember.

Andrew waits for "hope" to return to him.

There are many kinds of hope. There is hope that is based on falsehoods. Beth had hoped that Thad was alive. It was not hope based on reality. It was not hope based on evidence. It was a false hope that existed only because Beth's sanity could not co-exist with what she knew to be true.

Sandy believed that she could survive the death of her sister and her husband, because she chose hope. Chosen hope is a life choice; it is a personal statement that the future can be better because the individual chooses to believe that it can...and will be better. But it is more than just the act of choosing. It requires the individual to move forward making each decision a testament to better times.

Andrew's hope was a kind of inborn hope. It is the hope that exists when all other avenues have become dead ends. It is the hope that children are born with...it is the hope that thrives in the environment where there are no other possible outcomes. This hope stands in the face of all the other evidence that says that logical options have run their course.

There are some that believe that inborn hope is nothing more than foolish hope. Then there are others that believe that this form of hope is the bedrock of faith.

The End

ALWAYS THADDEUS

Book 2

(Please enjoy this sneak peek)

CHAPTER I

Petty Officer, Craig Hendershott is proud of his new rank as boatswain's mate, masters of seamanship or 'boats' as he calls his new title. The U. S. Coast guard had been good to him during his short tenure with them. He had recently been assigned to a Coast Guard Cutter, specifically a coastal buoy tender.

He loves to ride the cutter into the deeper waters, being responsible for performing almost any task in connection with deck maintenance, small boat operations, navigation, and especially his task of supervising all personnel assigned to a ship's deck force. It is an honor and he is proud. This cutter, his cutter, is responsible for the buoys off Maine's coast up and through the Bay of Fundy. At present, they are the cruising coastal waters approximately twenty miles from their homeport of Jonesport.

The crew had already navigated past the smaller islands off Maine's coast. Craig knew these waters well, and had boated around all the inlets and harbors as a teen. In fact, because of his love of these waters, he had decided to join the Coast Guard and luckily for him, he was recently assigned to this cutter.

The waters were rough today with the waves ranging from eight to ten feet high. They were just recently warned by the National Data Buoy Center (NDBC) about the presence of Right Whales in the area. Right Whales are rotund and are one of the longest whales that swim these waters; some reaching sixty feet long. They are migrating now, and prefer to stay close to the reefs and buoys. Being a protected species by the United States' Endangered Species Act, the Coast Guard Cutters in the area were made very aware of their presence.

There was a small craft advisory out and so the cutter was traveling at a slower than normal speed of ten knots. The Coast Guard never wanted to be responsible for injuring one of these beautiful creatures and had no interest in making the breaking news on Fox, so the captain continued their slower cruising speed.

With Weather Station #44027, Buoy #101, less than a mile ahead, Craig gets out his binoculars to watch for the endangered whales. He stands on the bow of the cutter.

He knows this particular buoy is bright yellow and stands about twenty feet above the surface. It contains every piece of weather equipment one would need to understand current conditions: the water temperature, wind speed, wave height, barometric pressure, air temp and other weather information.

Petty Officer Hendershott searches for the familiar buoy in his field of vision and soon spots it. He scans the waves to be certain that there were no right whales in the area. Looking more closely, he is sure he sees something on or near the buoy.

He radios the Chief Petty Officer his concerns, and they slow the cutter to five knots as to not disturb the whales, which he figures are swimming around the buoy.

But as the cutter gets closer to the buoy, his eyes begin to play tricks on him. He can see that there is something bright green on the buoy. It is not a Right Whale at all. As he refocuses his binoculars, he can make out a body lying on the buoy.

Radioing the bridge once again, he notifies his Commander of a change to a Search and Rescue mission. As they approach the buoy, he realizes that he is right. There is a body, a woman's body, lying on the buoy with no signs of life. She is wearing bright green clothing and a blood stained t-shirt.

As the crew goes into full rescue operations, a rescue helicopter is enlisted to help in their efforts. Performing training exercises in the area, the U.S. Coast Guard Rescue helicopter is able to arrive within ten minutes. Upon reaching the scene, the rescue swimmers waste no time jumping from the helicopter into the cold New England waters.

The woman looks to be very badly injured and unconscious to Craig. He watches intently from the deck as the swimmers reach the buoy and pull her safely onto the *Sked*. The stretcher is quickly raised up to the helicopter that is hovering fifty feet above the waves. Listening to her chest and feeling her pulse, the swimmer gives Craig and the cutter's crew a 'thumbs up' meaning that she is alive.

After the chopper retrieves their precious cargo and hauls her aboard, it quickly turns to fly towards the trauma unit in a hospital in Bangor, Maine.

Craig begins to relax as the cutter heads up towards the Bay of Fundy. He is proud of how he had performed in his newly acquired position. He would like to check up on the woman that he helped to save when he returns to base. He even hopes, that perhaps, he can go to the hospital and meet her.

Four days later, Craig Hendershott, heads to Bangor on his motorcycle. He is en route to the hospital where the woman he had discovered on the buoy is being treated. He found out before he left base that she was a 'Jane Doe'. Although she was conscious now, she has no recollection of her past and how she became injured and unconscious, and lying on a weather buoy, twenty miles off the coast of Maine. Her injuries included broken ribs and legs, a severe life-threatening concussion, and countless cuts and bruises on her face and arms.

When he arrives at the hospital, the nurses only give him a few minutes to sit with her. They tell him that she needs her rest as she is still suffering from a severe concussion. As he sits down beside the stranger, she smiles a wide smile up at him and grabs his hand before she falls back into a deep sleep.

Driving back to the base after his short visit with her, Petty Officer Hendershott can't get the woman and her smile out of his mind. He decides that he has to go back to see her again, when she is better. Jane Doe had made an impression on the young sailor and he couldn't shake a deep-seated feeling that he needed to help her.

ABOUT THE ARTIST

James Mackenzie is a widely exhibited English artist with a rapidly growing UK and international reputation. His expressionist series, 'Skyscapes' is particularly collectable.

He gained his Fine Art (Hons) Degree at Hertfordshire University in 2000. After his Degree, he worked as a portrait artist for a time before deciding to study for a Post Graduate Certificate in Education in Art and Design.

He went on to teach Art in secondary education for several years. During his time teaching he continued to paint and experiment with a wide range of styles and techniques. In recent years, James has discovered the style about which he is most passionate. He describes it as a 'natural' style of painting. This 'natural' almost spontaneous painting style allows his subconscious to take hold and he is able to create seascapes and landscapes, which previously existed only as memories or unconscious recollection.

James is passionate about his creation of seascapes, as he feels that there is so much power and energy in the sea juxtaposed against its periodic peace and tranquility. His technique with these pieces is to let the paint almost guide how the painting will form. He changes the angle of the canvas and runs water over sections of it as part of the process of creation. During this process, he says that often as much paint is removed from the canvas as remains as part of the composition. James is often asked to produce commissions for his clients and his seascapes have become extremely sought after.

The artwork for the cover of 'Always Thaddeus' comes from a previously commissioned piece that James had already completed when he began talking with Marcee Corn. She greatly admired the artist's work and had purchased two pieces previously. Together, they decided that one of his seascapes would work nicely for the cover of *Always Thaddeus* after she sent him a portion of her manuscript, describing the 'unforgiving' and 'wild' sea.

Mr. Mackenzie also created the sketches within the book. Ms. Corn had provided James with photographs of the Maine coastline and also detailed descriptions of the scenes she envisioned. The touchstone for the lighthouse in the first sketch was a beautiful drawing, created by Robert E. Lee Stokes - Marcee's father.

James works on his art full-time from his studio in Essex, where he is often joined by his young son Liam, who, with his own small easel, seems set to follow in his father's artistic footsteps. James is married to Ruth and, with Liam; they spend as much family time together as possible, enjoying holidays, day trips to London as well as time in the local countryside.

Since establishing his full time artistic career he has exhibited in many renowned galleries including, most recently, a solo exhibition at the prestigious Lloyd's Resister building, in the City of London. His paintings are in great demand. Limited edition prints taken from his paintings, including the cover artwork for *Always Thaddeus* are available. Please visit:

www.mackenzieart.co.uk

Lightning Source UK Ltd.
Milton Keynes UK
UKOW04f2153020817
306549UK00001B/57/P